ELMHURST PUBLIC LIBRARY

3 1135 01859 1401

S0-ARK-830

J
GN
STOKER

DRACULA

Adapted by
Daniel Conner

Illustrated by
Rod Espinosa

Based upon the works of
Bram Stoker

magic
Wagon

visit us at
www.abdopublishing.com

Published by Magic Wagon, a division of the ABDO Group, 8000 West 78th Street, Edina, Minnesota 55439. Copyright © 2010 by Abdo Consulting Group, Inc. International copyrights reserved in all countries. All rights reserved. No part of this book may be reproduced in any form without written permission from the publisher.

Graphic Planet™ is a trademark and logo of Magic Wagon.

Printed in the United States.

 Manufactured with paper containing at least 10% post-consumer waste

Original novel by Bram Stoker
Adapted by Daniel Conner
Illustrated by Rod Espinosa
Edited by Stephanie Hedlund and Rochelle Baltzer
Interior layout and design by Antarctic Press
Cover art by Rod Espinosa
Cover design by Neil Klinepier

Library of Congress Cataloging-in-Publication Data

Conner, Daniel, 1985-
    Dracula / adapted by Daniel Conner ; illustrated by Rod Espinosa ; based
    upon the works of Bram Stoker.
        p. cm. -- (Graphic planet. Graphic horror)
    Summary: A graphic novel based on the Bram Stoker classic, in which young
    Jonathan Harker first meets and then must destroy Count Dracula in order to
    save those closest to him.
    ISBN 978-1-60270-676-7 (alk. paper)
    1. Graphic novels. [1. Graphic novels. 2. Vampires--Fiction. 3.
    Transylvania (Romania)--Fiction. 4. Youths' writings. 5. Horror stories. 6.
    Stoker, Bram, 1847-1912. Dracula--Adaptations.] I. Espinosa, Rod, ill. II.
    Stoker, Bram, 1847-1912. Dracula. III. Title.

PZ7.7.C66Dr 2010
741.5'973--dc22

                                                                2009008584

TABLE OF CONTENTS

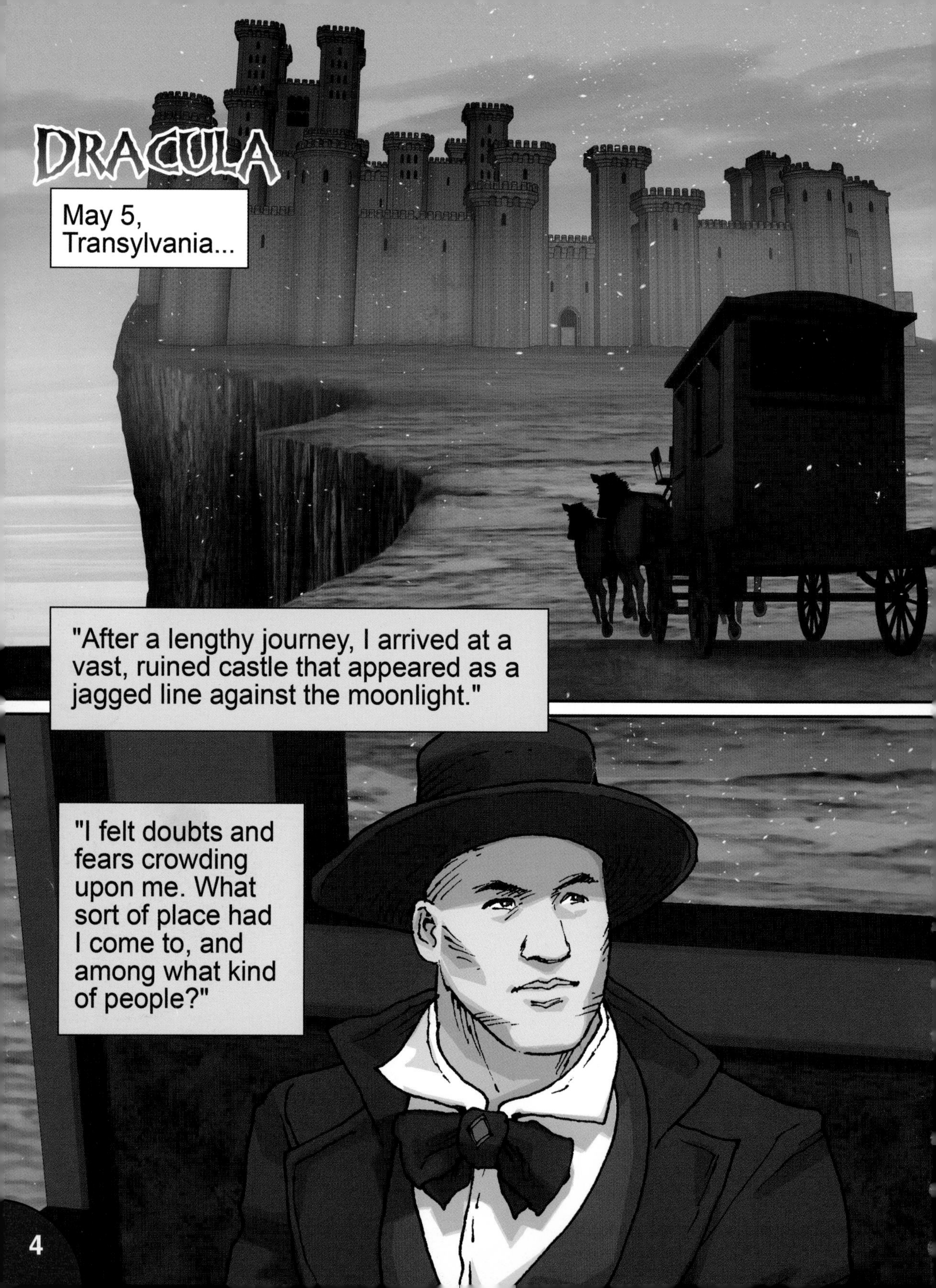
DRACULA
May 5, Transylvania...
"After a lengthy journey, I arrived at a vast, ruined castle that appeared as a jagged line against the moonlight."
"I felt doubts and fears crowding upon me. What sort of place had I come to, and among what kind of people?"

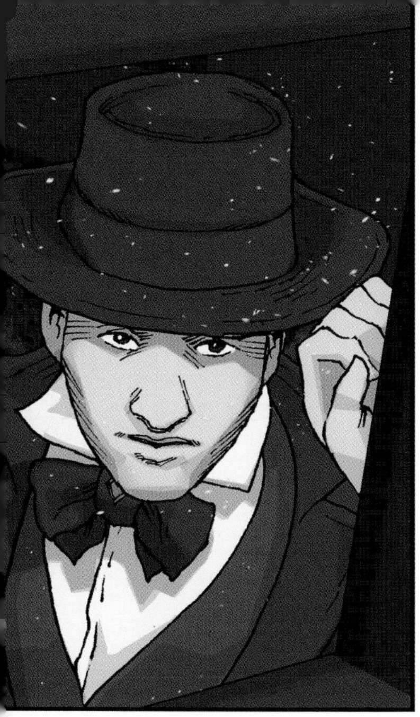

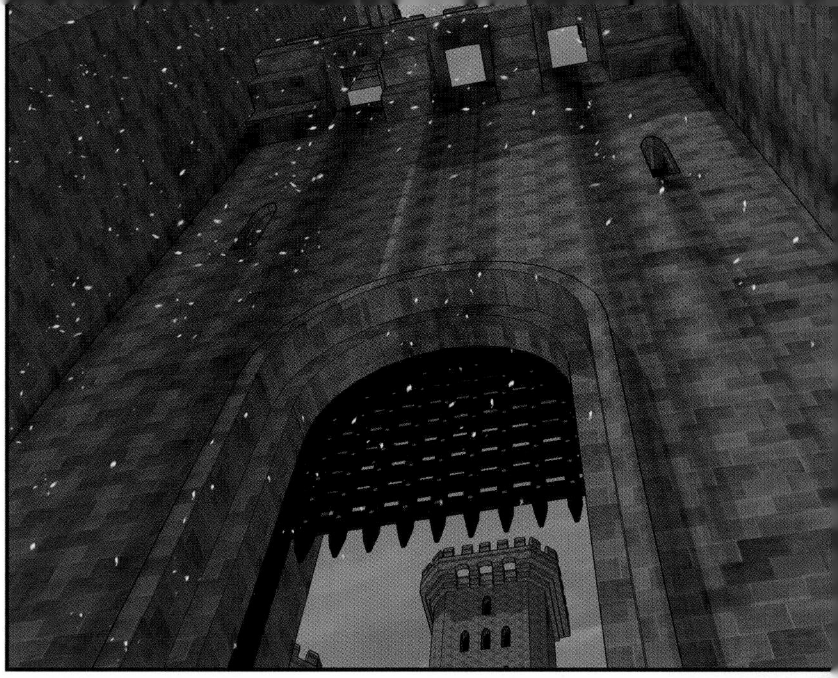

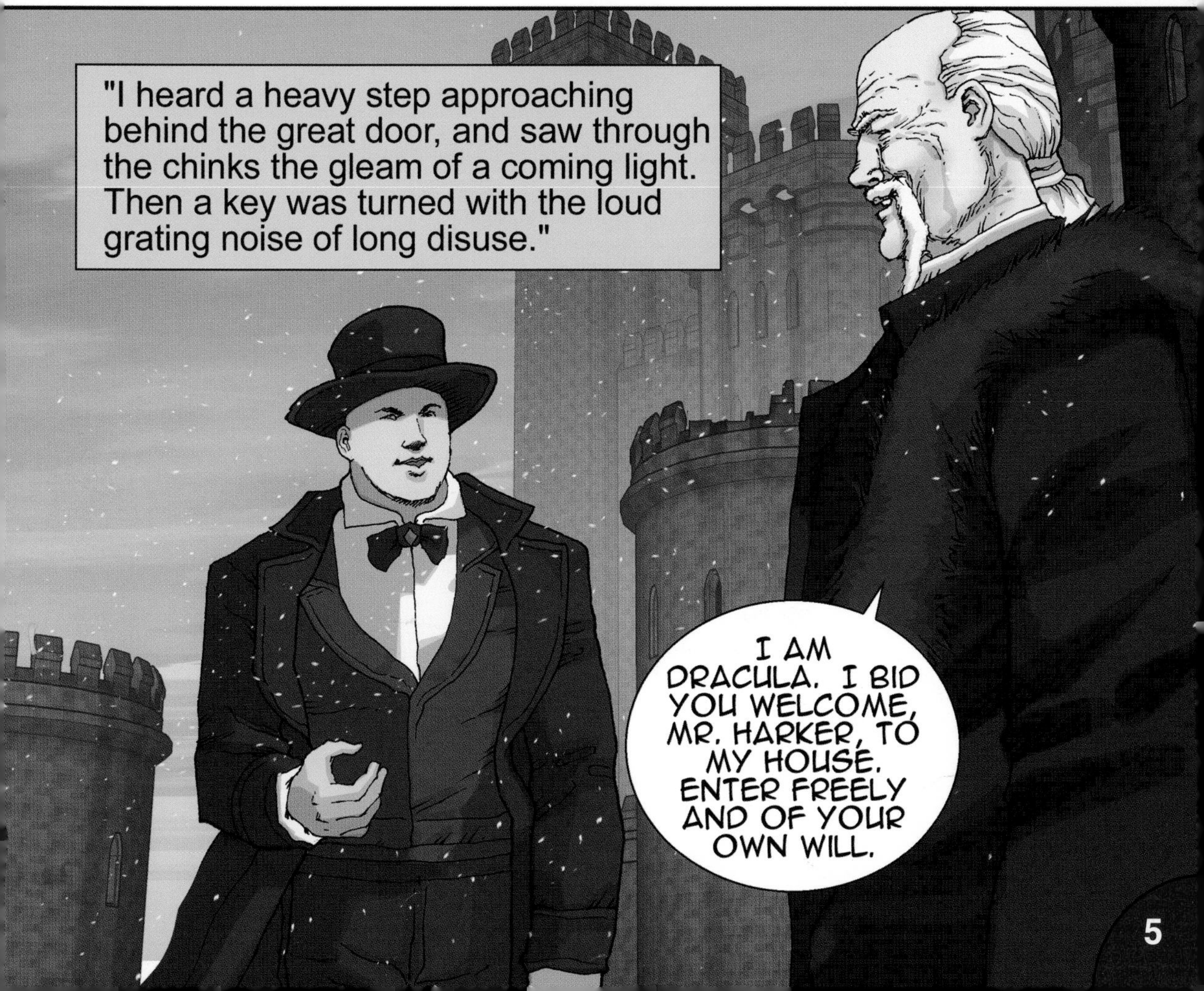
"I heard a heavy step approaching behind the great door, and saw through the chinks the gleam of a coming light. Then a key was turned with the loud grating noise of long disuse."
I AM DRACULA. I BID YOU WELCOME, MR. HARKER, TO MY HOUSE. ENTER FREELY AND OF YOUR OWN WILL.

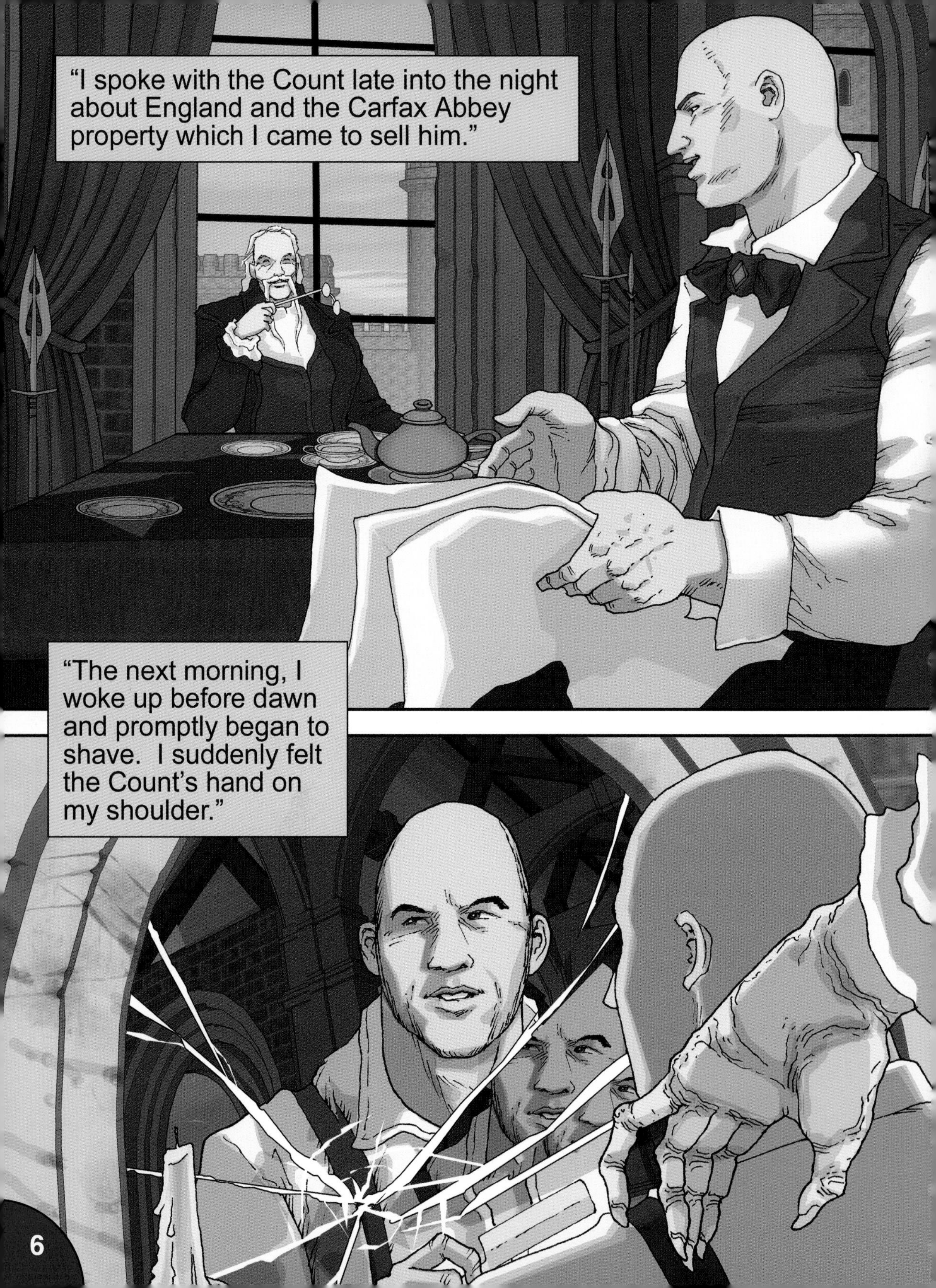
"I spoke with the Count late into the night about England and the Carfax Abbey property which I came to sell him."
"The next morning, I woke up before dawn and promptly began to shave. I suddenly felt the Count's hand on my shoulder."

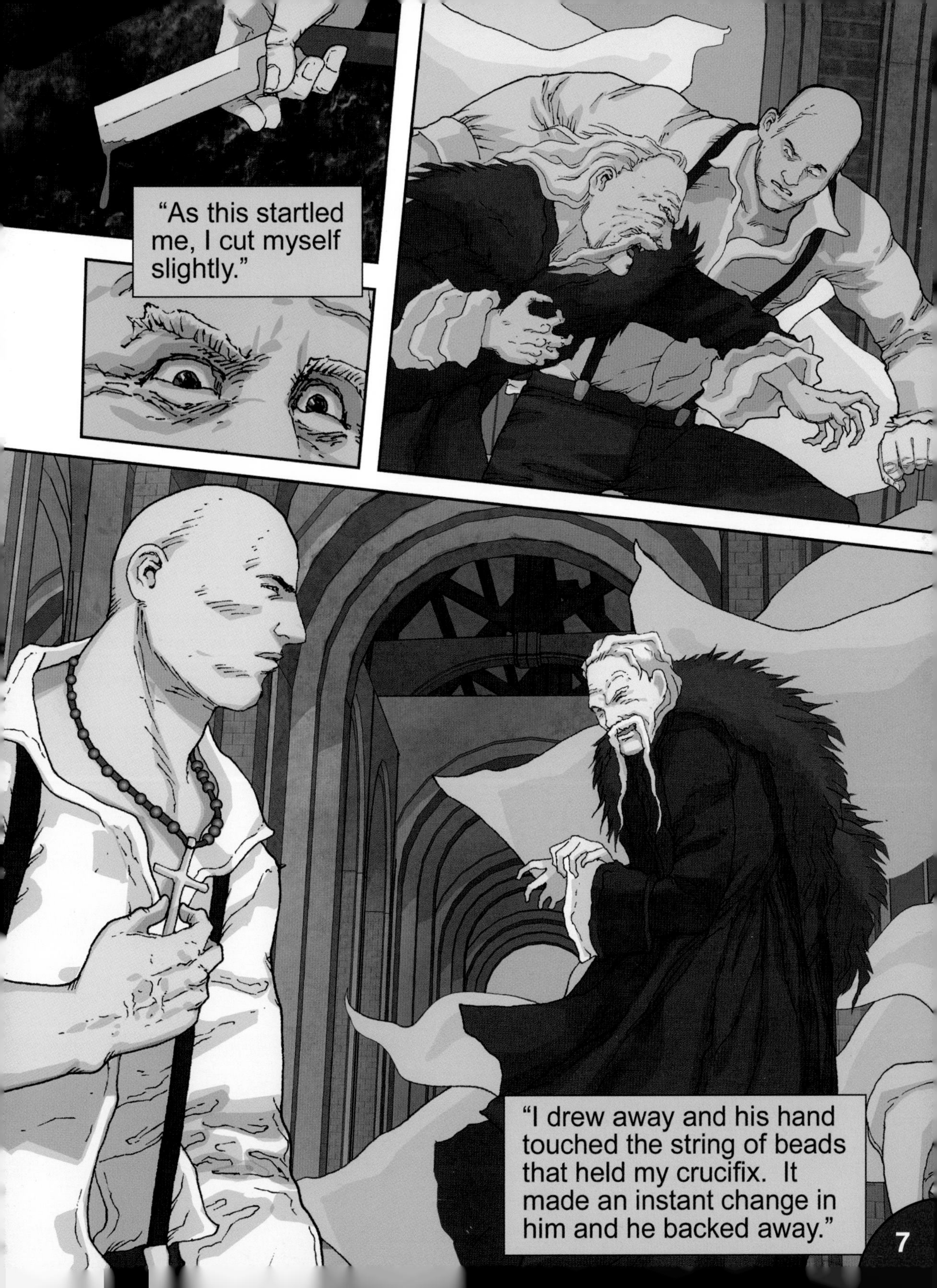
"As this startled me, I cut myself slightly."
"I drew away and his hand touched the string of beads that held my crucifix. It made an instant change in him and he backed away."

"I have seen no servants or people other than the Count. Surely, he and I cannot be alone."

"I have continued to explore this castle, which is beginning to feel like a prison. In a basement, I found a large wooden box filled with dirt. Inside it lay the Count!"

"A few days have passed, and today I have seen the strangest sight yet. I saw the Count emerge from a window and crawl down the castle wall, facedown! What manner of creature is this?"

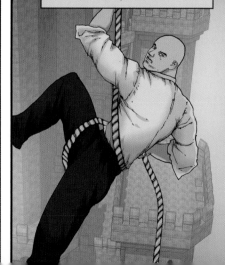

"I resolved to find a way home from this dreadful place."

May 9, London...

"My dearest Lucy, forgive my delay in writing, I have been preparing for my marriage to Jonathan. Although, I have hardly heard anything from him while he has been in Transylvania."

MY DEAREST MINA, THANKS FOR YOUR SWEET LETTER! HERE AM I, 19 YEARS OLD, AND I HAVE NEVER HAD A PROPOSAL TILL TODAY.

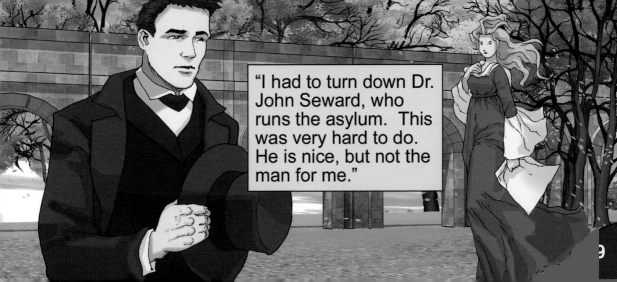

"I had to turn down Dr. John Seward, who runs the asylum. This was very hard to do. He is nice, but not the man for me."

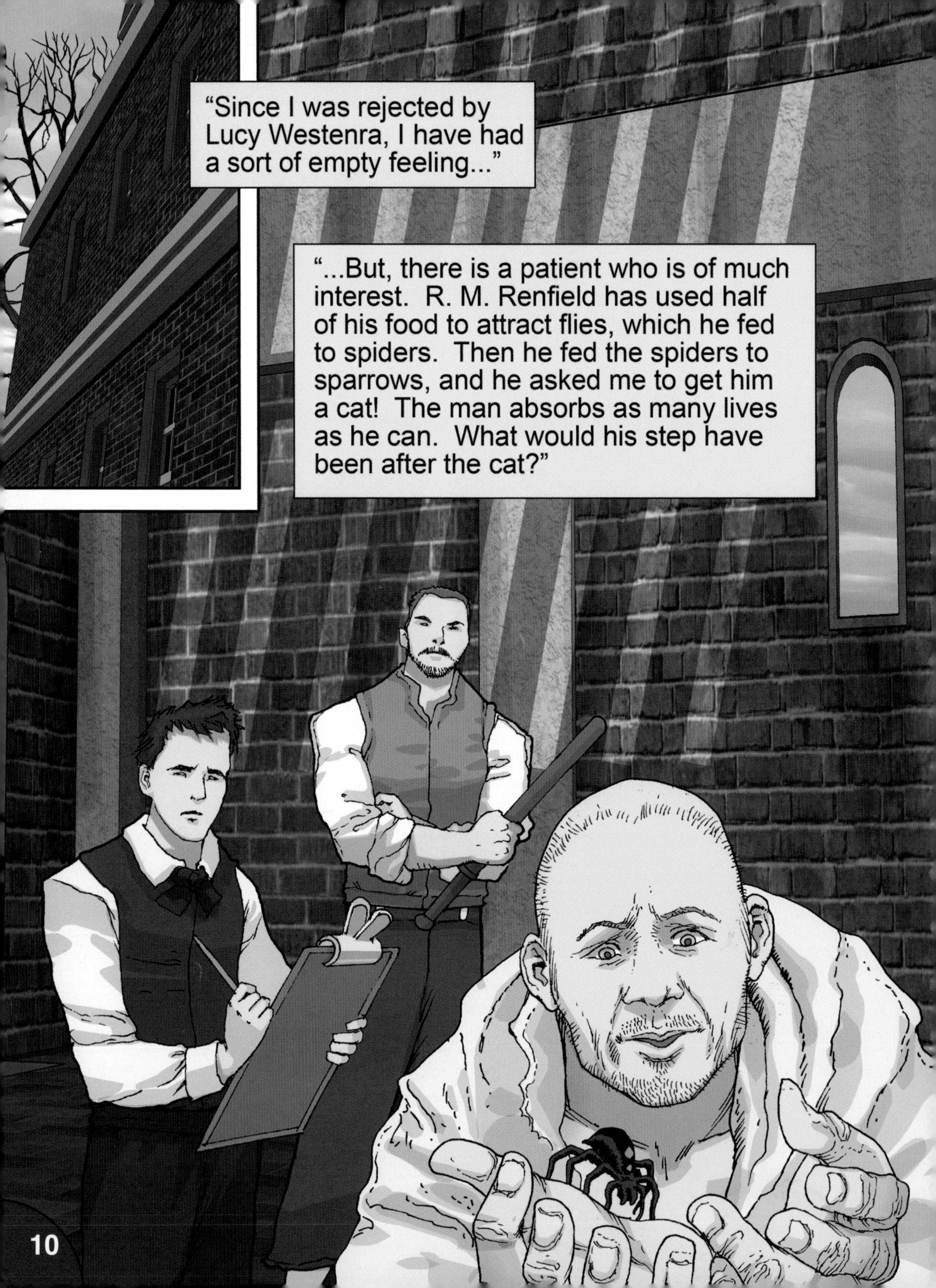
"Since I was rejected by Lucy Westenra, I have had a sort of empty feeling..."
"...But, there is a patient who is of much interest. R. M. Renfield has used half of his food to attract flies, which he fed to spiders. Then he fed the spiders to sparrows, and he asked me to get him a cat! The man absorbs as many lives as he can. What would his step have been after the cat?"

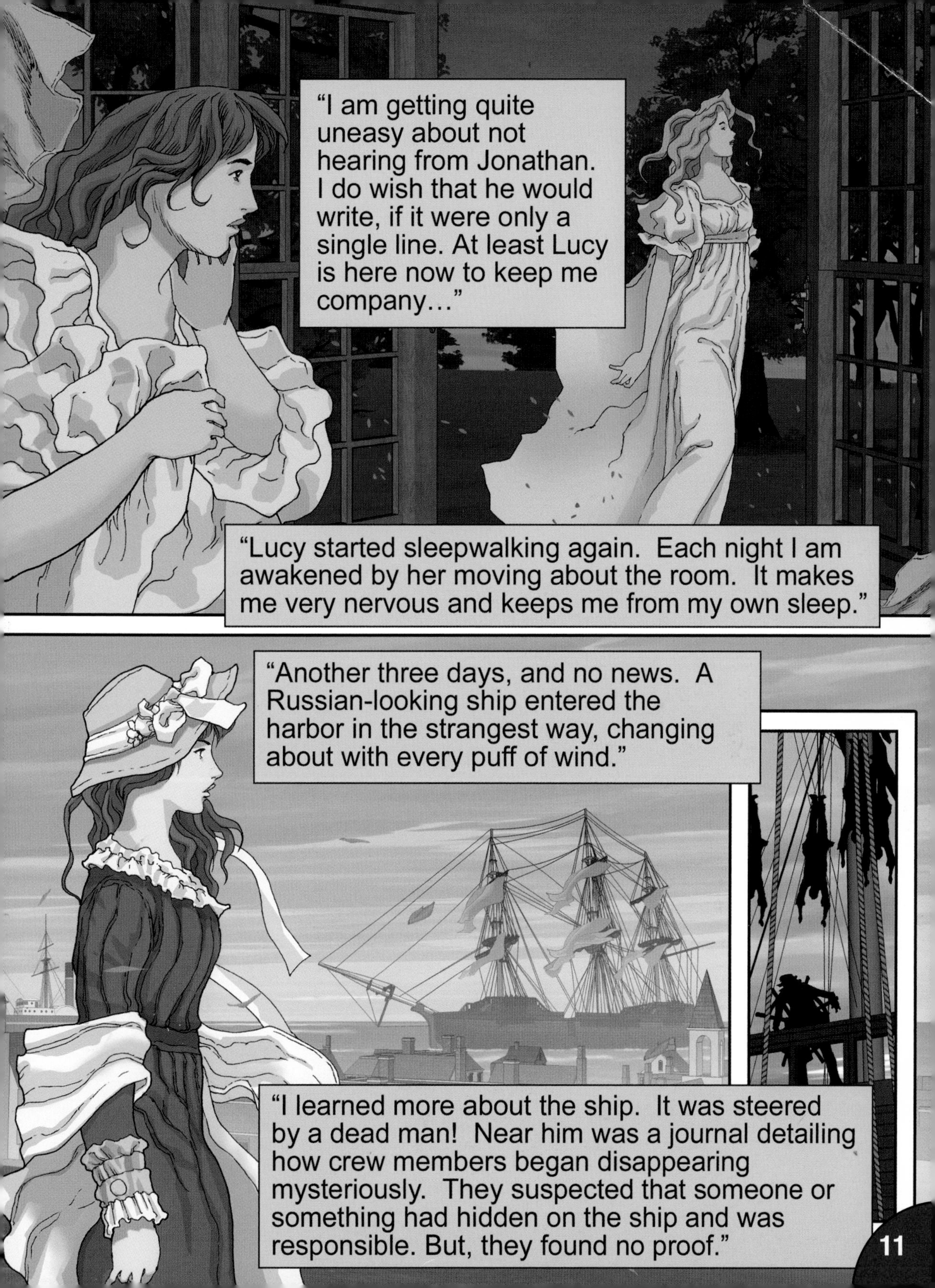
"I am getting quite uneasy about not hearing from Jonathan. I do wish that he would write, if it were only a single line. At least Lucy is here now to keep me company…"
"Lucy started sleepwalking again. Each night I am awakened by her moving about the room. It makes me very nervous and keeps me from my own sleep."
"Another three days, and no news. A Russian-looking ship entered the harbor in the strangest way, changing about with every puff of wind."
"I learned more about the ship. It was steered by a dead man! Near him was a journal detailing how crew members began disappearing mysteriously. They suspected that someone or something had hidden on the ship and was responsible. But, they found no proof."

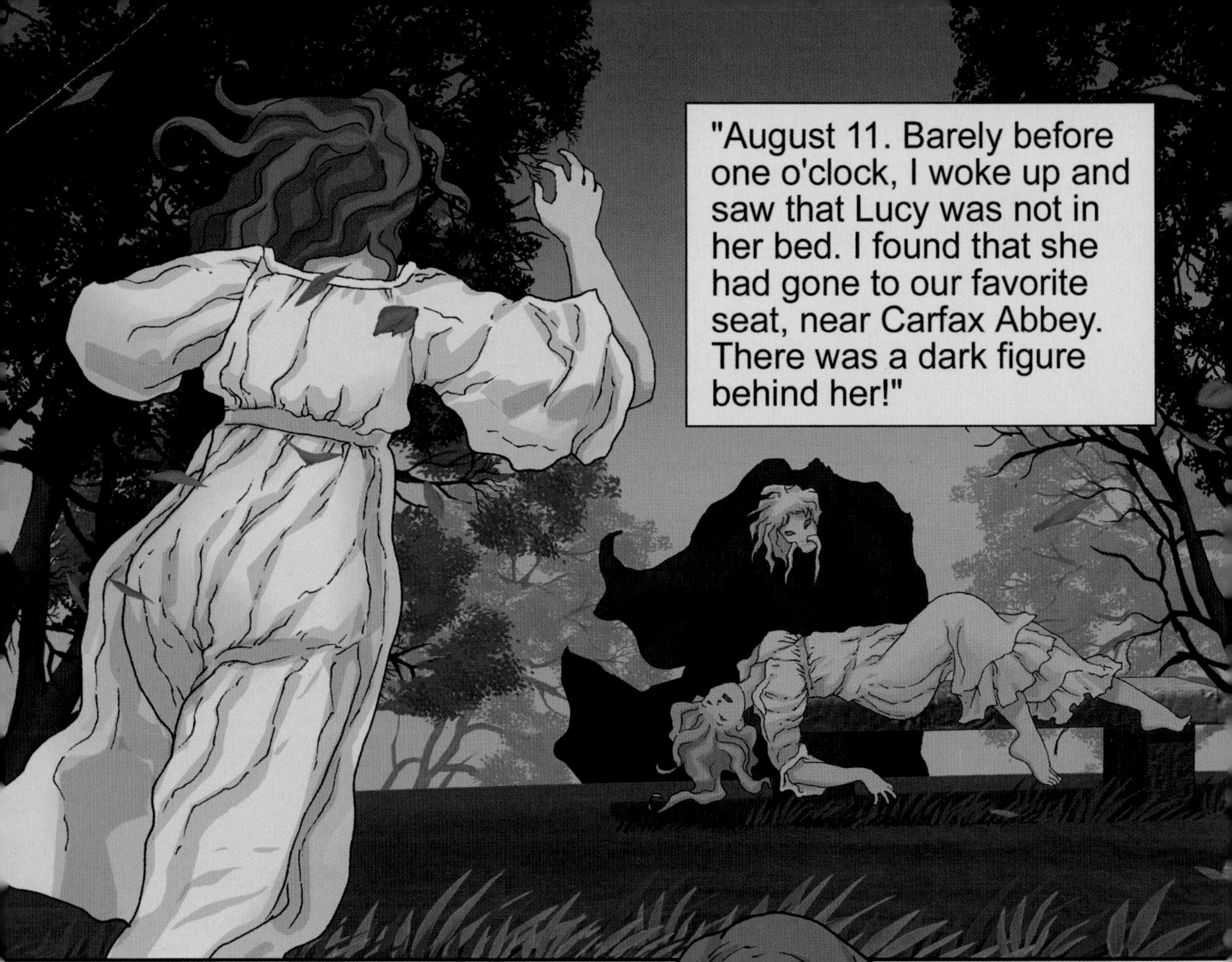
"August 11. Barely before one o'clock, I woke up and saw that Lucy was not in her bed. I found that she had gone to our favorite seat, near Carfax Abbey. There was a dark figure behind her!"

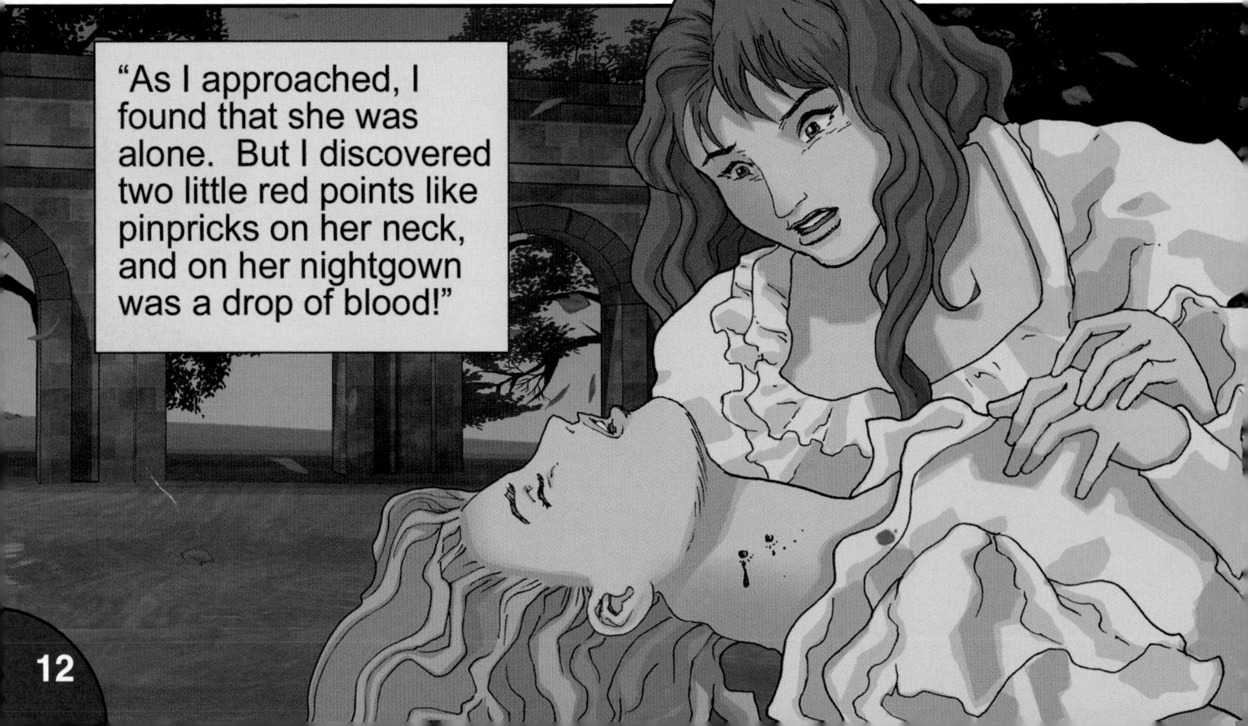
"As I approached, I found that she was alone. But I discovered two little red points like pinpricks on her neck, and on her nightgown was a drop of blood!"

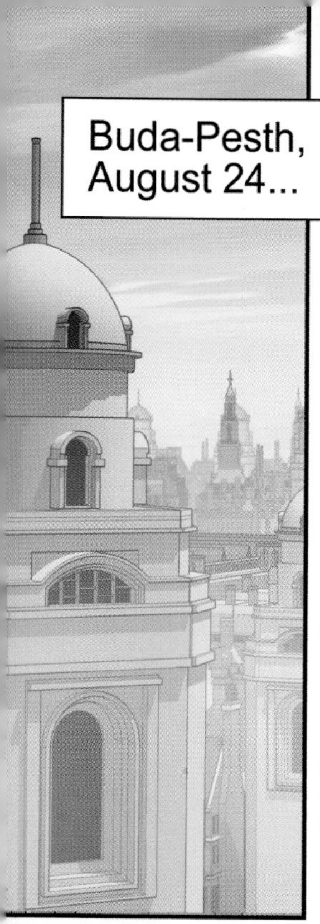
Buda-Pesth, August 24...

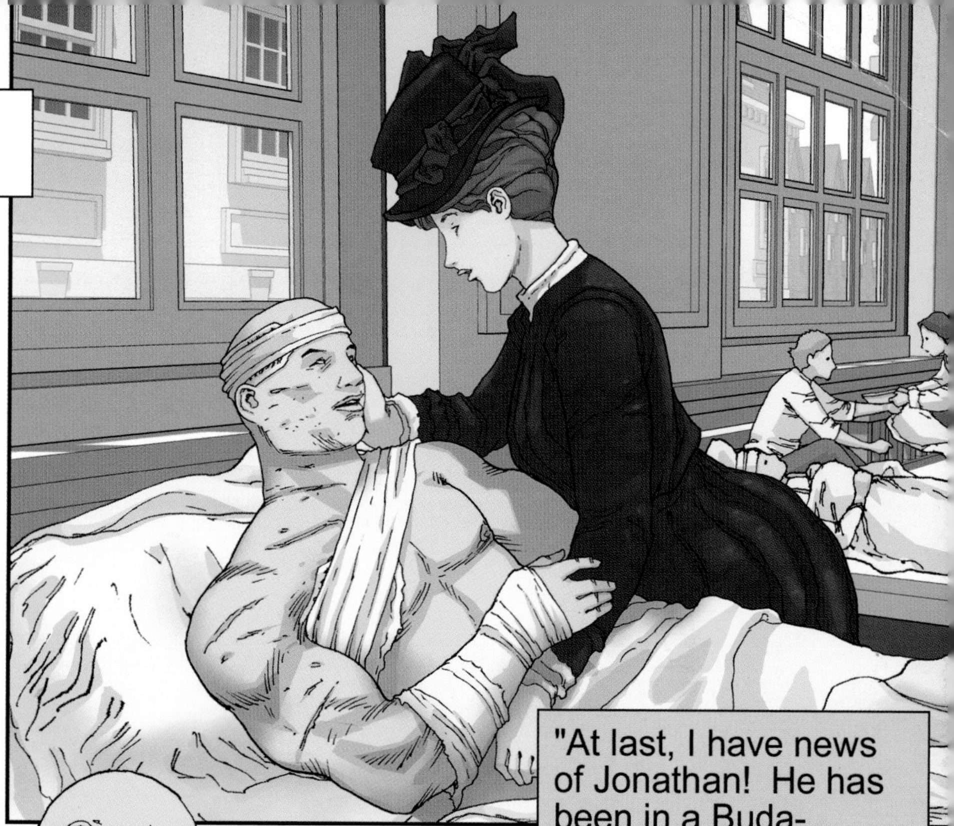
"At last, I have news of Jonathan! He has been in a Buda-Pesth hospital for six weeks! I am now at his bedside."

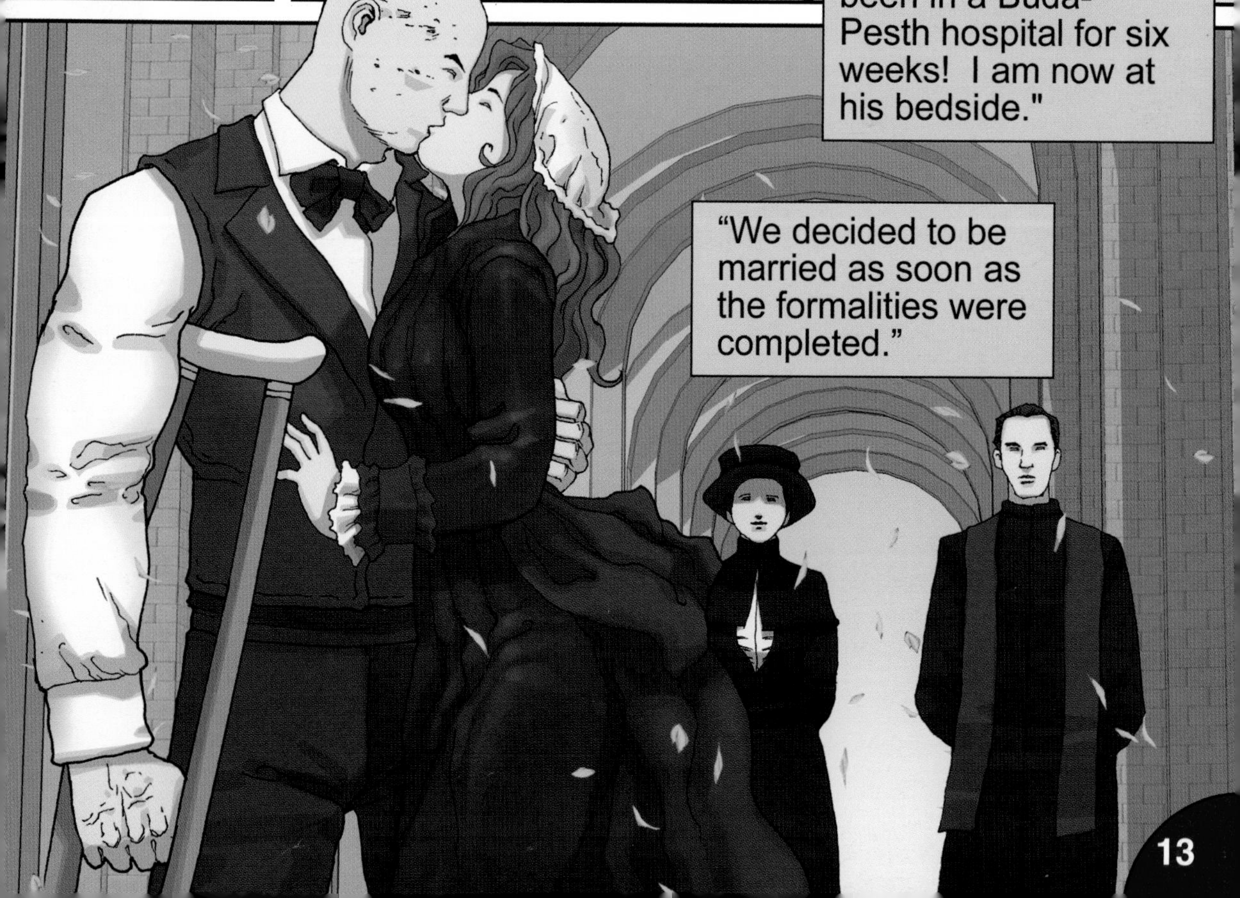
“We decided to be married as soon as the formalities were completed.”

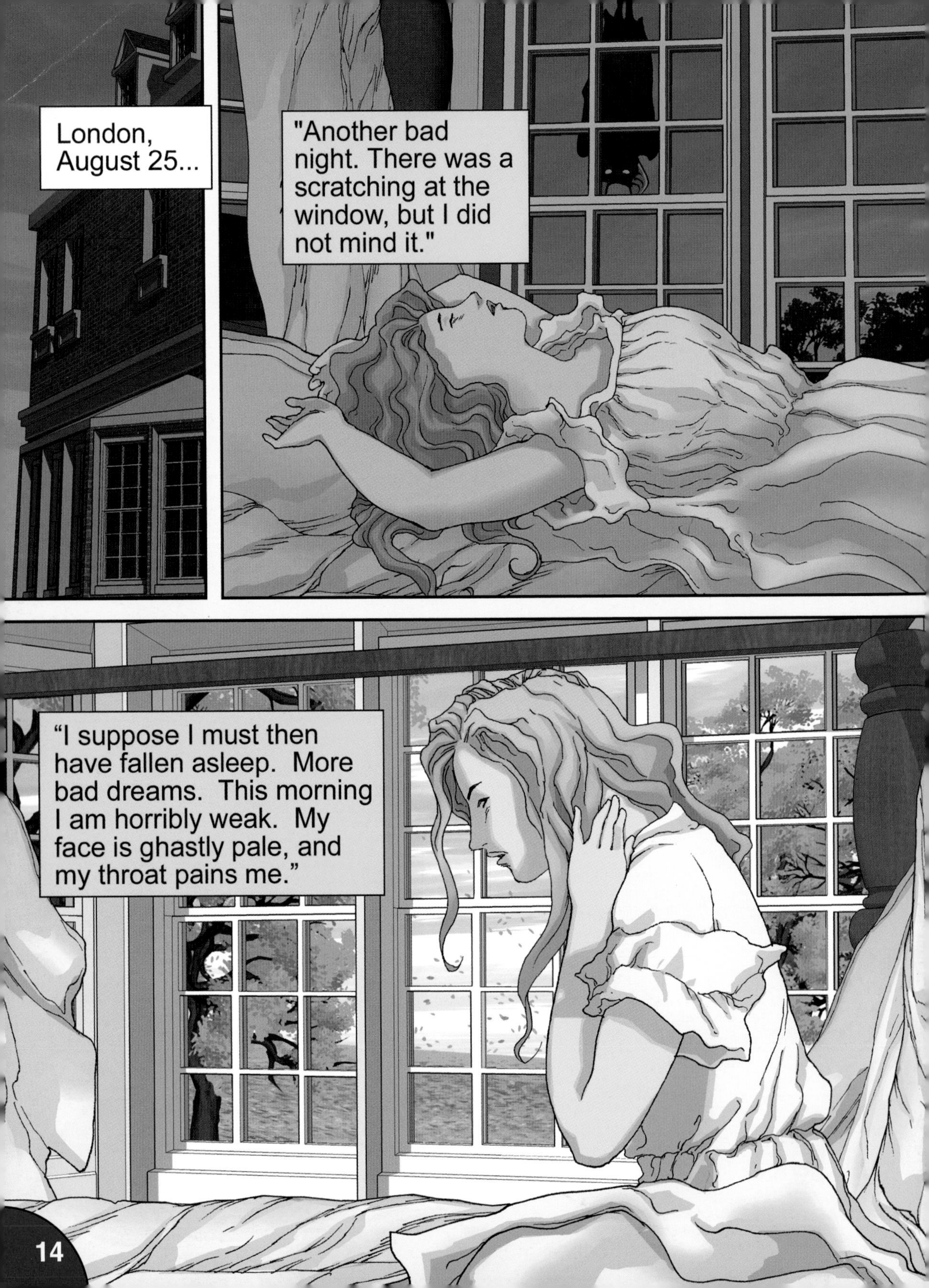
London, August 25...
"Another bad night. There was a scratching at the window, but I did not mind it."
"I suppose I must then have fallen asleep. More bad dreams. This morning I am horribly weak. My face is ghastly pale, and my throat pains me."

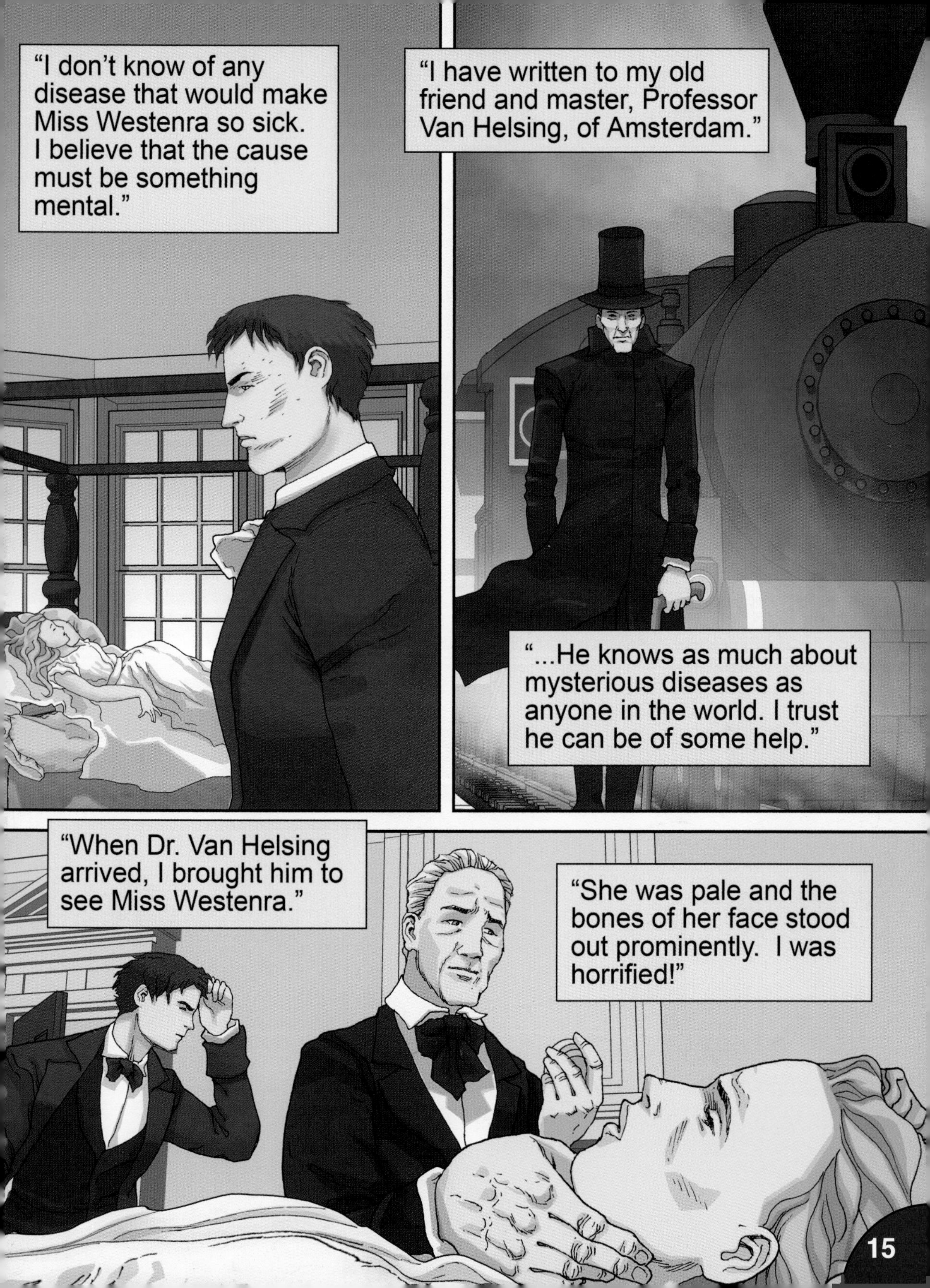
"I don't know of any disease that would make Miss Westenra so sick. I believe that the cause must be something mental."
"I have written to my old friend and master, Professor Van Helsing, of Amsterdam."
"...He knows as much about mysterious diseases as anyone in the world. I trust he can be of some help."
"When Dr. Van Helsing arrived, I brought him to see Miss Westenra."
"She was pale and the bones of her face stood out prominently. I was horrified!"

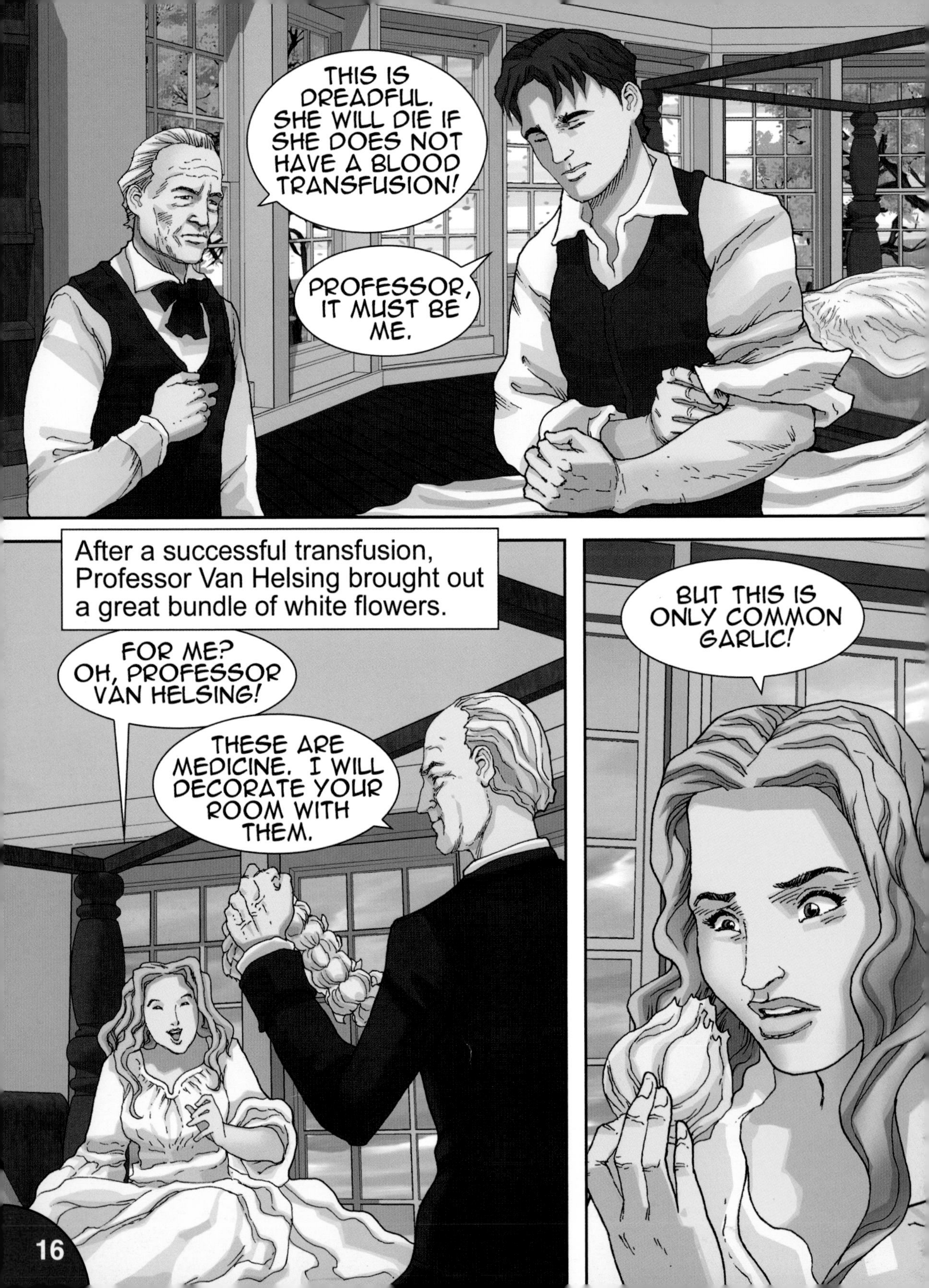
THIS IS DREADFUL. SHE WILL DIE IF SHE DOES NOT HAVE A BLOOD TRANSFUSION!
PROFESSOR, IT MUST BE ME.
After a successful transfusion, Professor Van Helsing brought out a great bundle of white flowers.
FOR ME? OH, PROFESSOR VAN HELSING!
THESE ARE MEDICINE. I WILL DECORATE YOUR ROOM WITH THEM.
BUT THIS IS ONLY COMMON GARLIC!

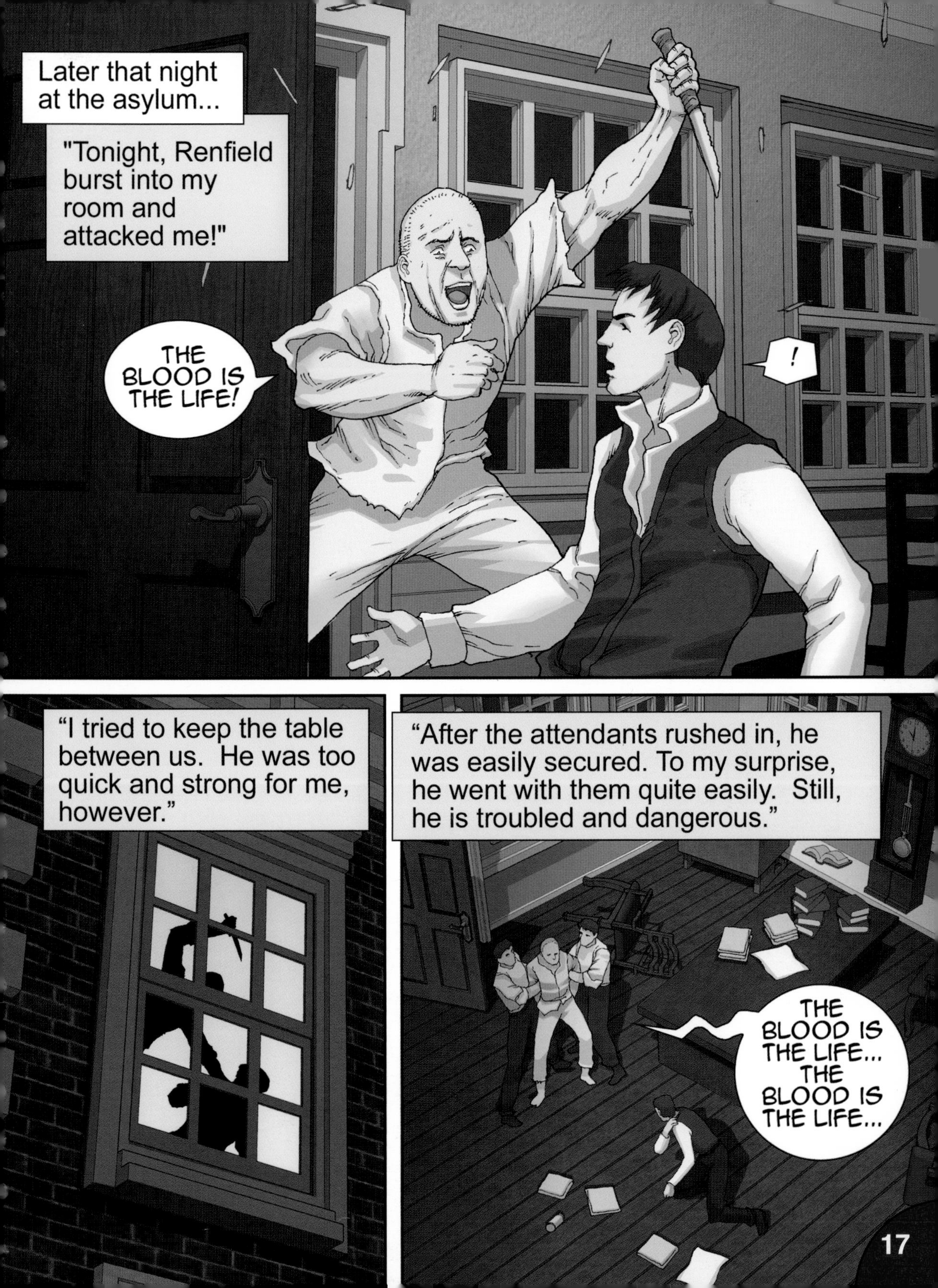
Later that night at the asylum...
"Tonight, Renfield burst into my room and attacked me!"
THE BLOOD IS THE LIFE!
!
"I tried to keep the table between us. He was too quick and strong for me, however."
"After the attendants rushed in, he was easily secured. To my surprise, he went with them quite easily. Still, he is troubled and dangerous."
THE BLOOD IS THE LIFE... THE BLOOD IS THE LIFE...

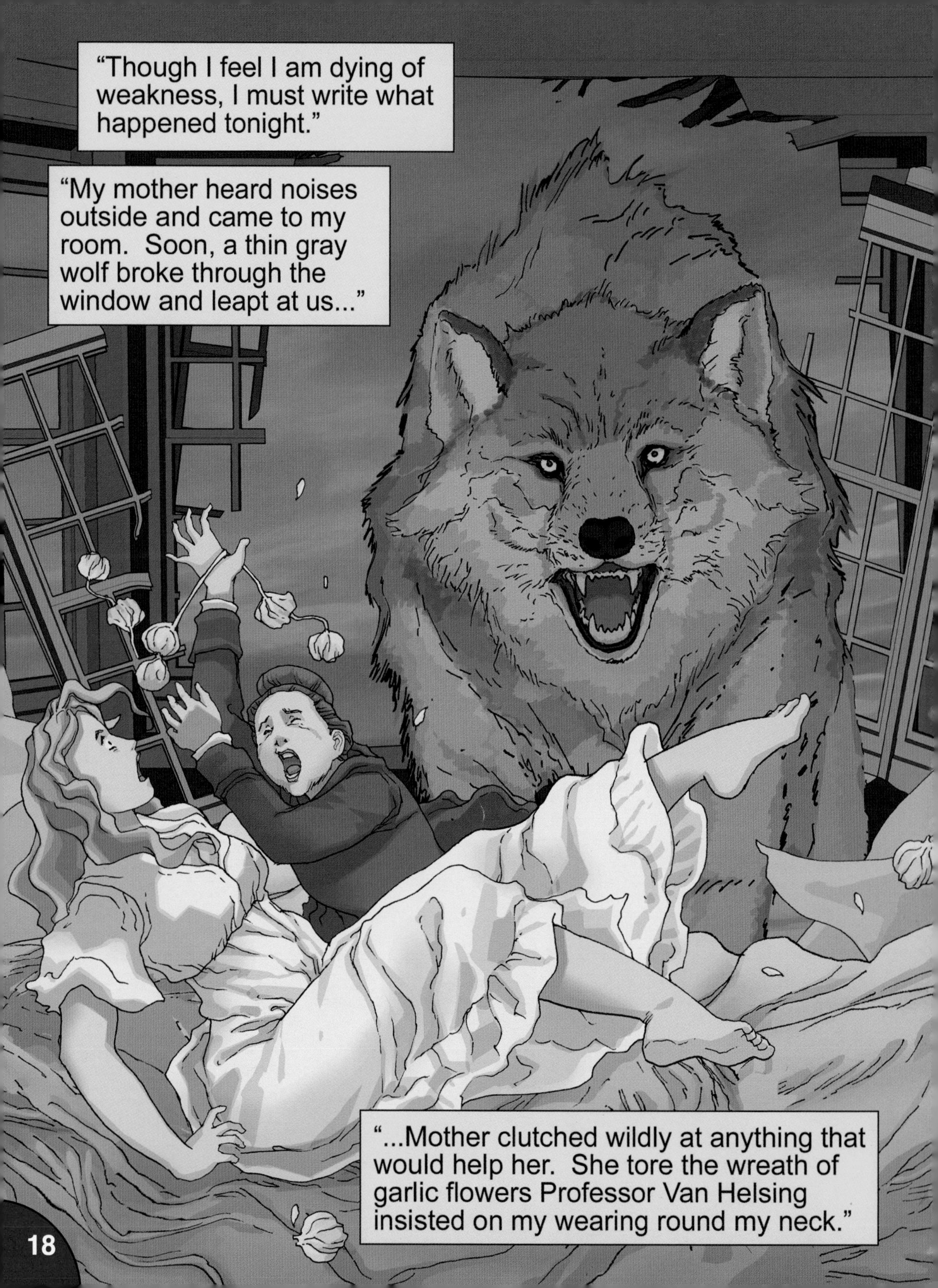
"Though I feel I am dying of weakness, I must write what happened tonight."
"My mother heard noises outside and came to my room. Soon, a thin gray wolf broke through the window and leapt at us..."
"...Mother clutched wildly at anything that would help her. She tore the wreath of garlic flowers Professor Van Helsing insisted on my wearing round my neck."

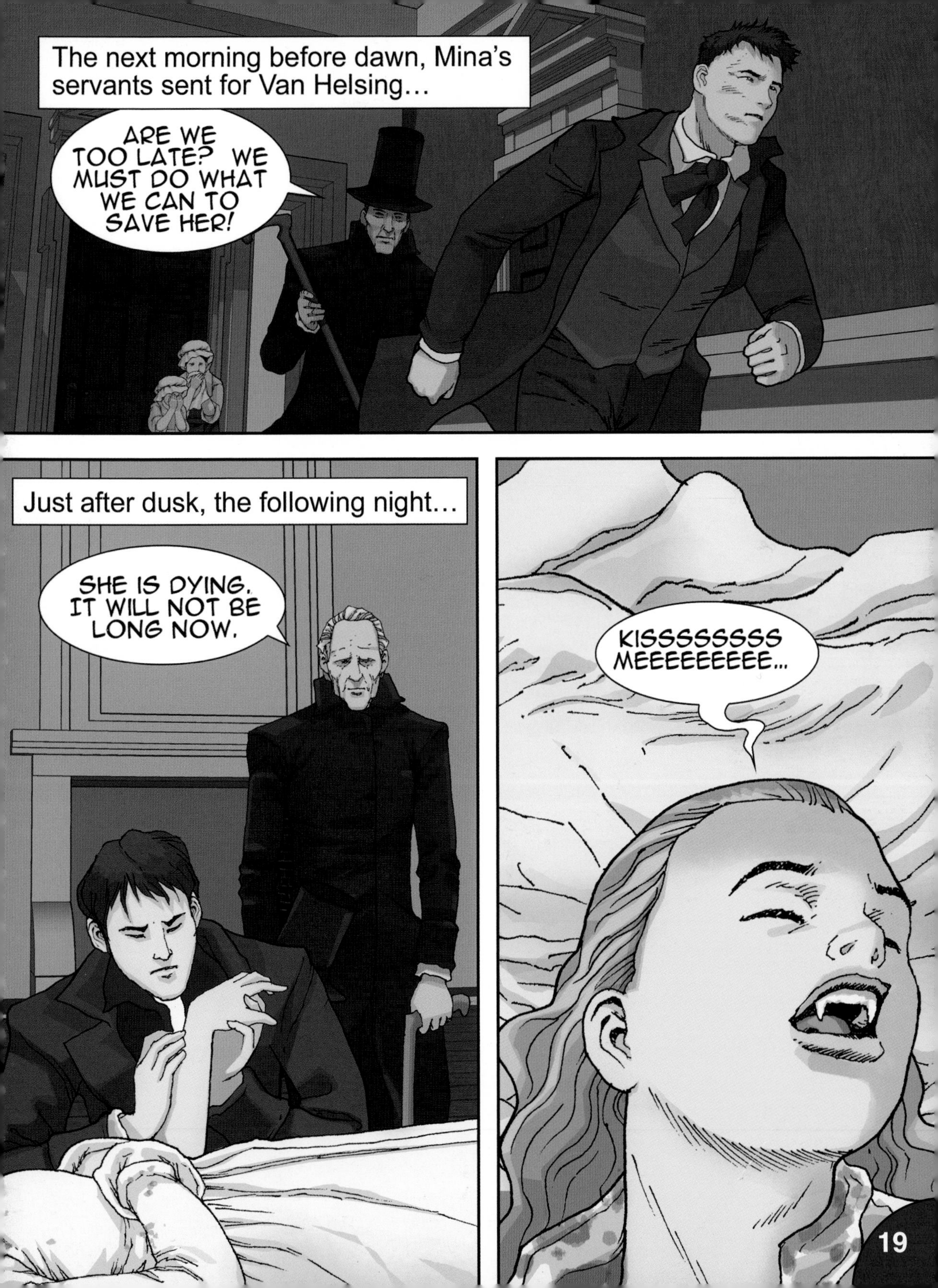

The next morning before dawn, Mina's servants sent for Van Helsing…
ARE WE TOO LATE? WE MUST DO WHAT WE CAN TO SAVE HER!
Just after dusk, the following night…
SHE IS DYING. IT WILL NOT BE LONG NOW.
KISSSSSSSS MEEEEEEEEE...

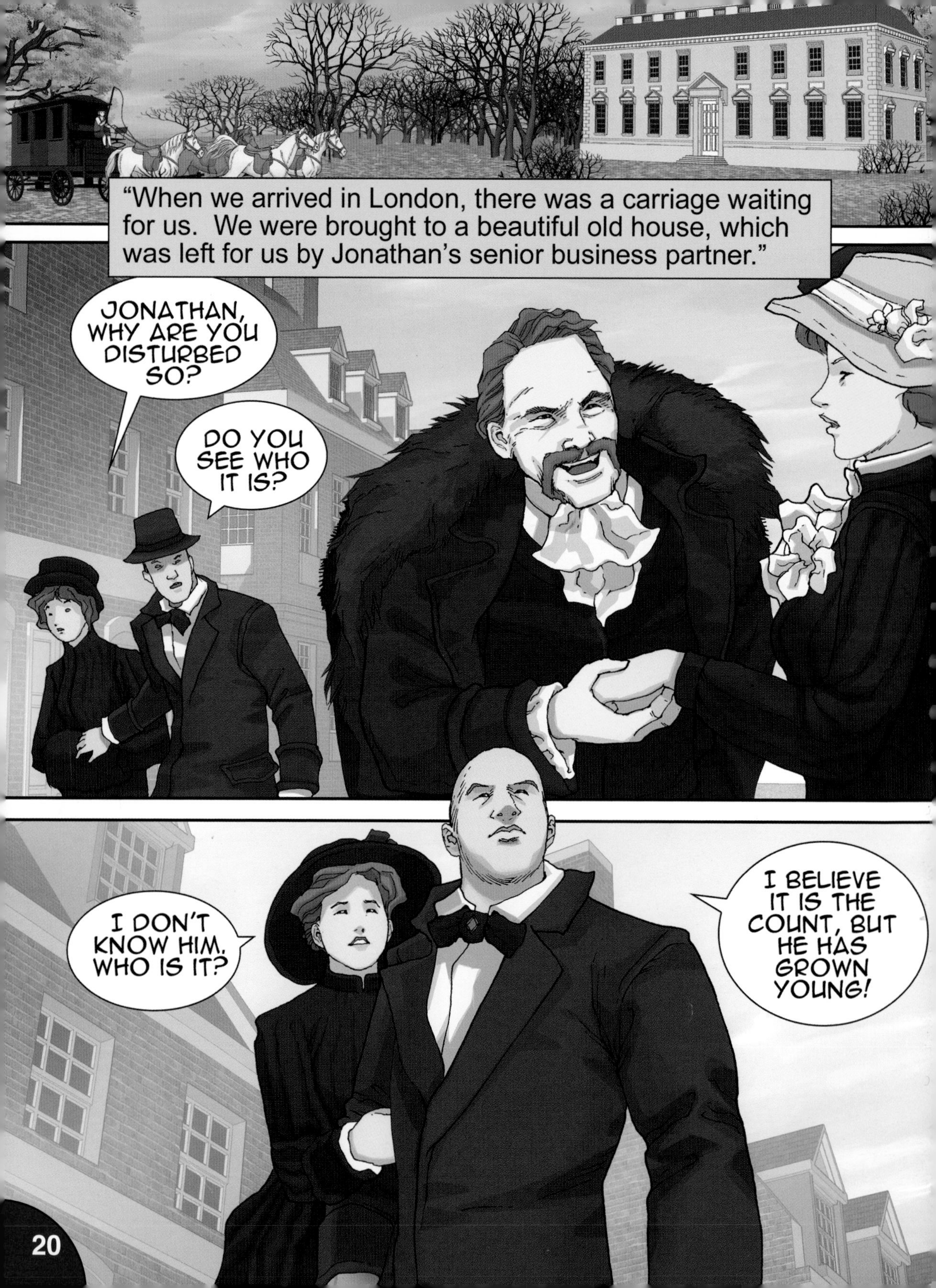
"When we arrived in London, there was a carriage waiting for us. We were brought to a beautiful old house, which was left for us by Jonathan's senior business partner."
JONATHAN, WHY ARE YOU DISTURBED SO?
DO YOU SEE WHO IT IS?
I DON'T KNOW HIM. WHO IS IT?
I BELIEVE IT IS THE COUNT, BUT HE HAS GROWN YOUNG!

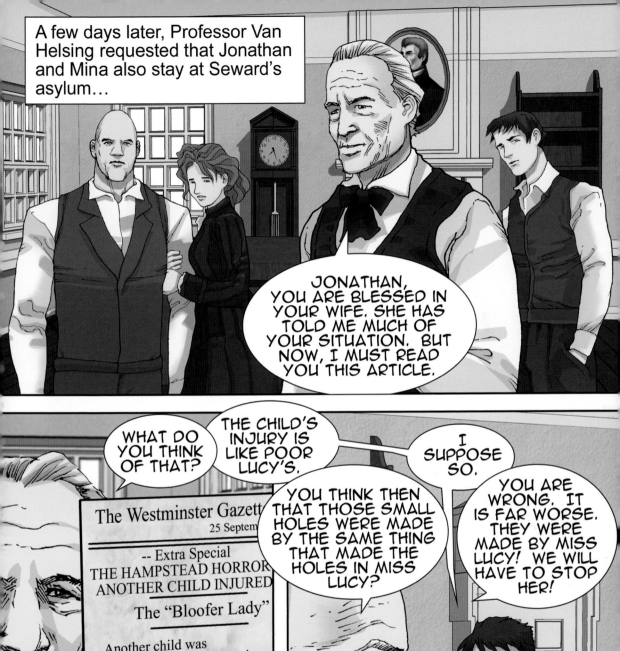

A few days later, Professor Van Helsing requested that Jonathan and Mina also stay at Seward's asylum…

JONATHAN, YOU ARE BLESSED IN YOUR WIFE. SHE HAS TOLD ME MUCH OF YOUR SITUATION. BUT NOW, I MUST READ YOU THIS ARTICLE.

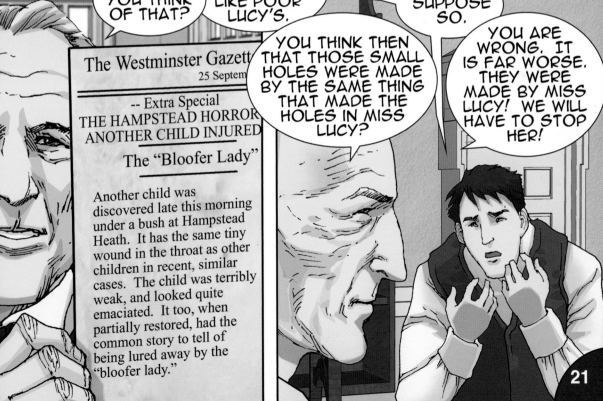

WHAT DO YOU THINK OF THAT?

THE CHILD'S INJURY IS LIKE POOR LUCY'S.

I SUPPOSE SO.

YOU THINK THEN THAT THOSE SMALL HOLES WERE MADE BY THE SAME THING THAT MADE THE HOLES IN MISS LUCY?

YOU ARE WRONG. IT IS FAR WORSE. THEY WERE MADE BY MISS LUCY! WE WILL HAVE TO STOP HER!

The Westminster Gazett

25 Septem

-- Extra Special
THE HAMPSTEAD HORROR
ANOTHER CHILD INJURED

The "Bloofer Lady"

Another child was discovered late this morning under a bush at Hampstead Heath. It has the same tiny wound in the throat as other children in recent, similar cases. The child was terribly weak, and looked quite emaciated. It too, when partially restored, had the common story to tell of being lured away by the "bloofer lady."

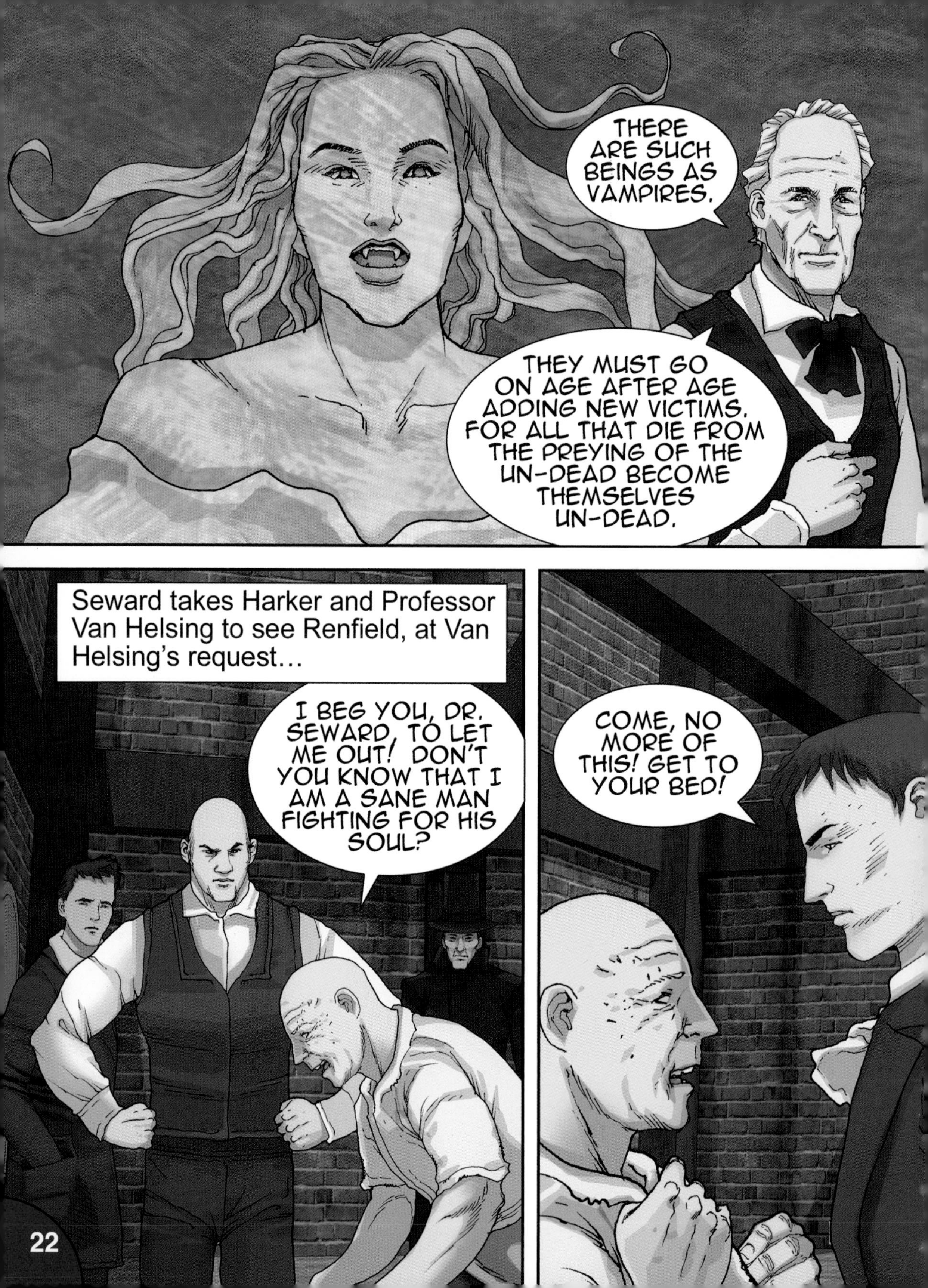
THERE ARE SUCH BEINGS AS VAMPIRES.
THEY MUST GO ON AGE AFTER AGE ADDING NEW VICTIMS. FOR ALL THAT DIE FROM THE PREYING OF THE UN-DEAD BECOME THEMSELVES UN-DEAD.
Seward takes Harker and Professor Van Helsing to see Renfield, at Van Helsing's request…
I BEG YOU, DR. SEWARD, TO LET ME OUT! DON'T YOU KNOW THAT I AM A SANE MAN FIGHTING FOR HIS SOUL?
COME, NO MORE OF THIS! GET TO YOUR BED!

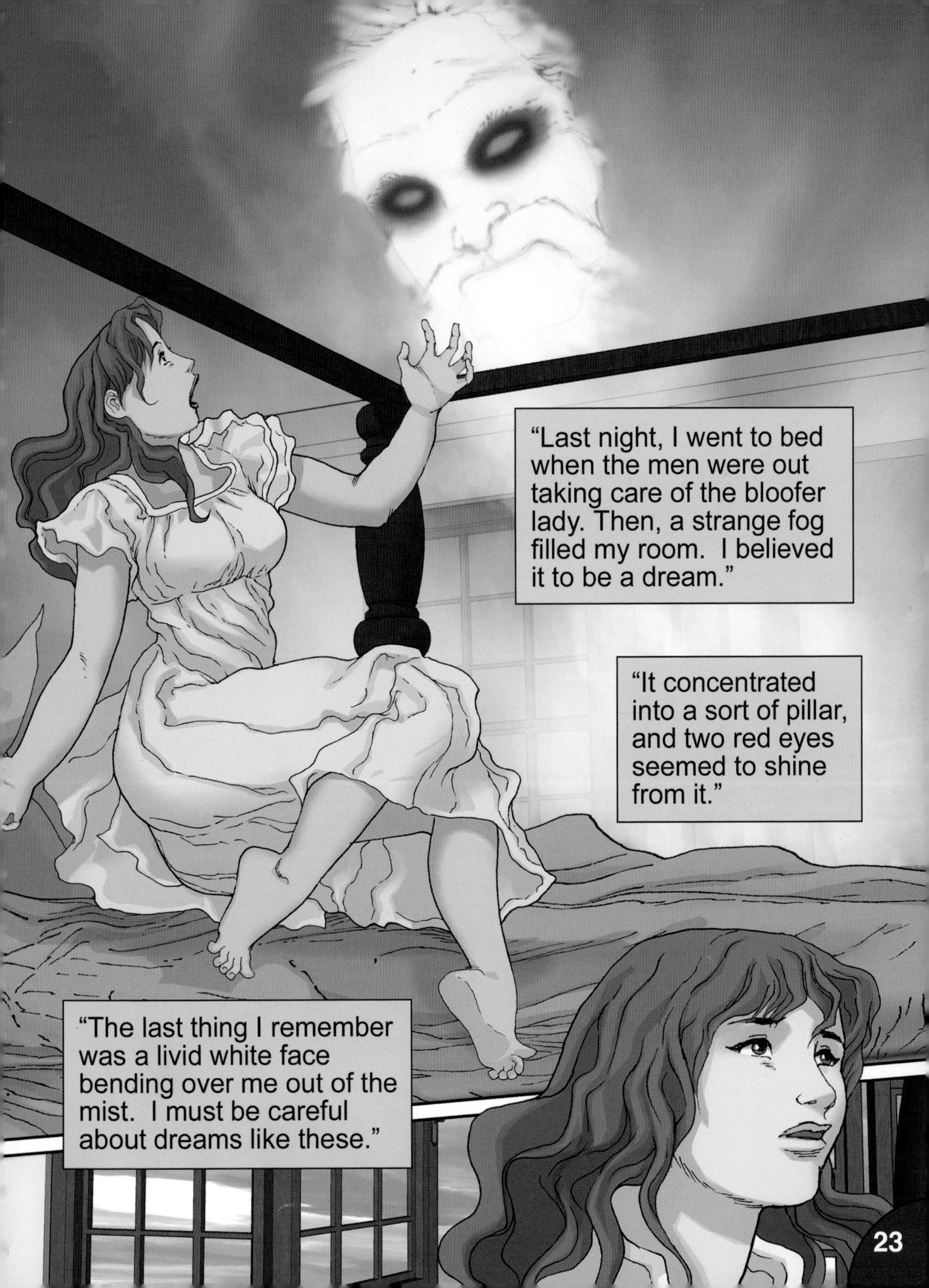
"Last night, I went to bed when the men were out taking care of the bloofer lady. Then, a strange fog filled my room. I believed it to be a dream."
"It concentrated into a sort of pillar, and two red eyes seemed to shine from it."
"The last thing I remember was a livid white face bending over me out of the mist. I must be careful about dreams like these."

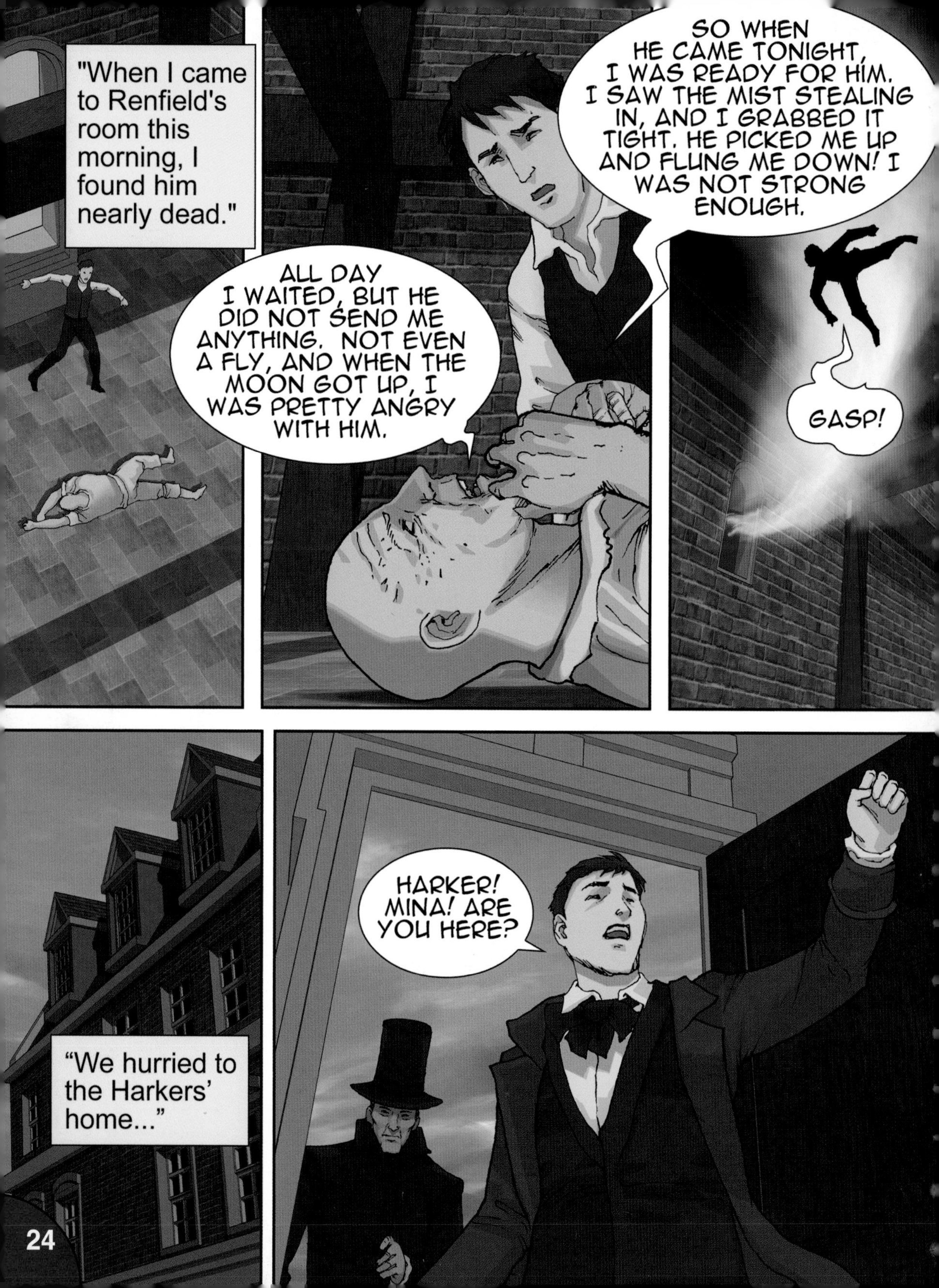
"When I came to Renfield's room this morning, I found him nearly dead."
ALL DAY I WAITED, BUT HE DID NOT SEND ME ANYTHING. NOT EVEN A FLY, AND WHEN THE MOON GOT UP, I WAS PRETTY ANGRY WITH HIM.
SO WHEN HE CAME TONIGHT, I WAS READY FOR HIM. I SAW THE MIST STEALING IN, AND I GRABBED IT TIGHT. HE PICKED ME UP AND FLUNG ME DOWN! I WAS NOT STRONG ENOUGH.
GASP!
"We hurried to the Harkers' home..."
HARKER! MINA! ARE YOU HERE?

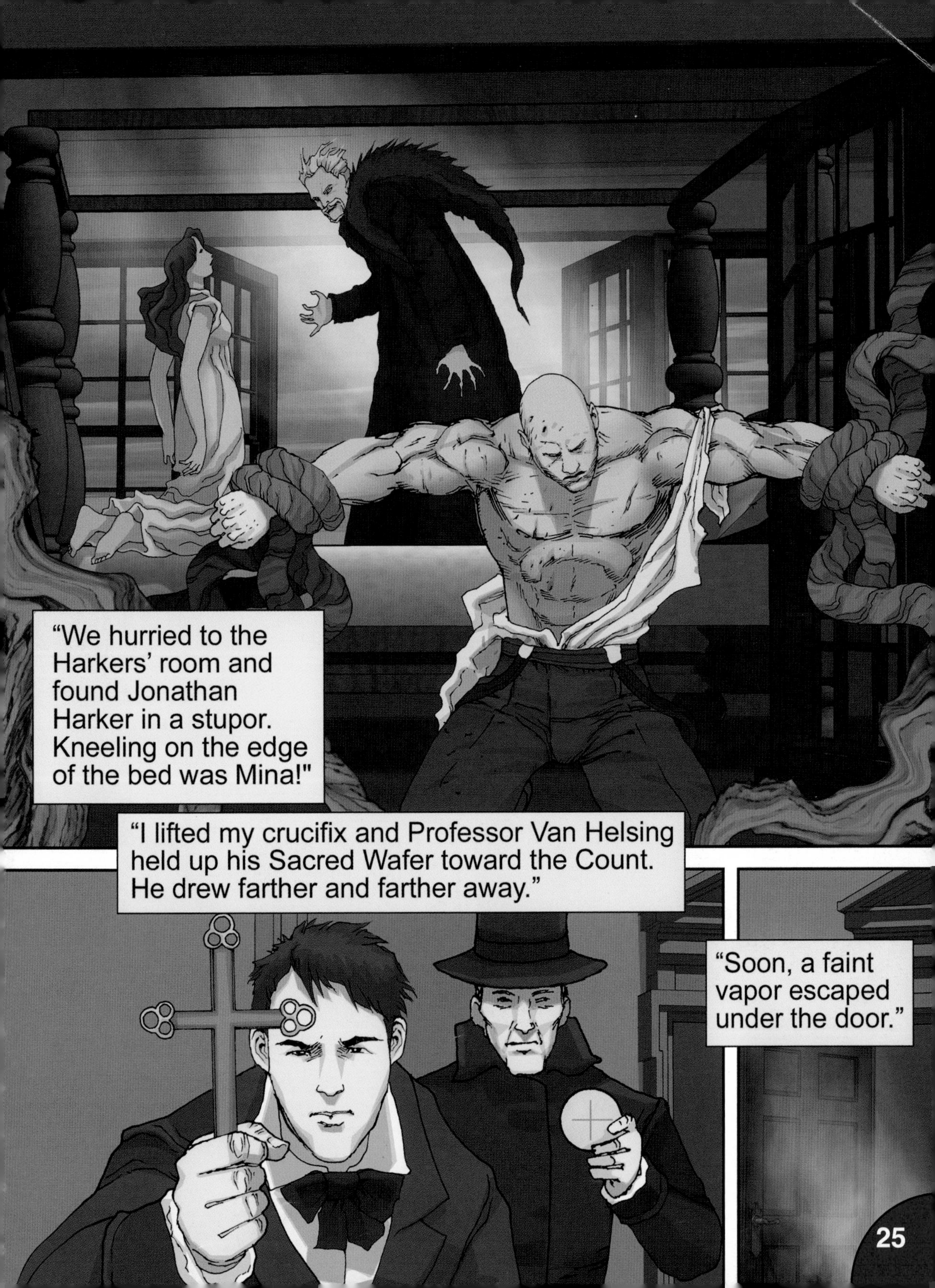
"We hurried to the Harkers' room and found Jonathan Harker in a stupor. Kneeling on the edge of the bed was Mina!"
"I lifted my crucifix and Professor Van Helsing held up his Sacred Wafer toward the Count. He drew farther and farther away."
"Soon, a faint vapor escaped under the door."

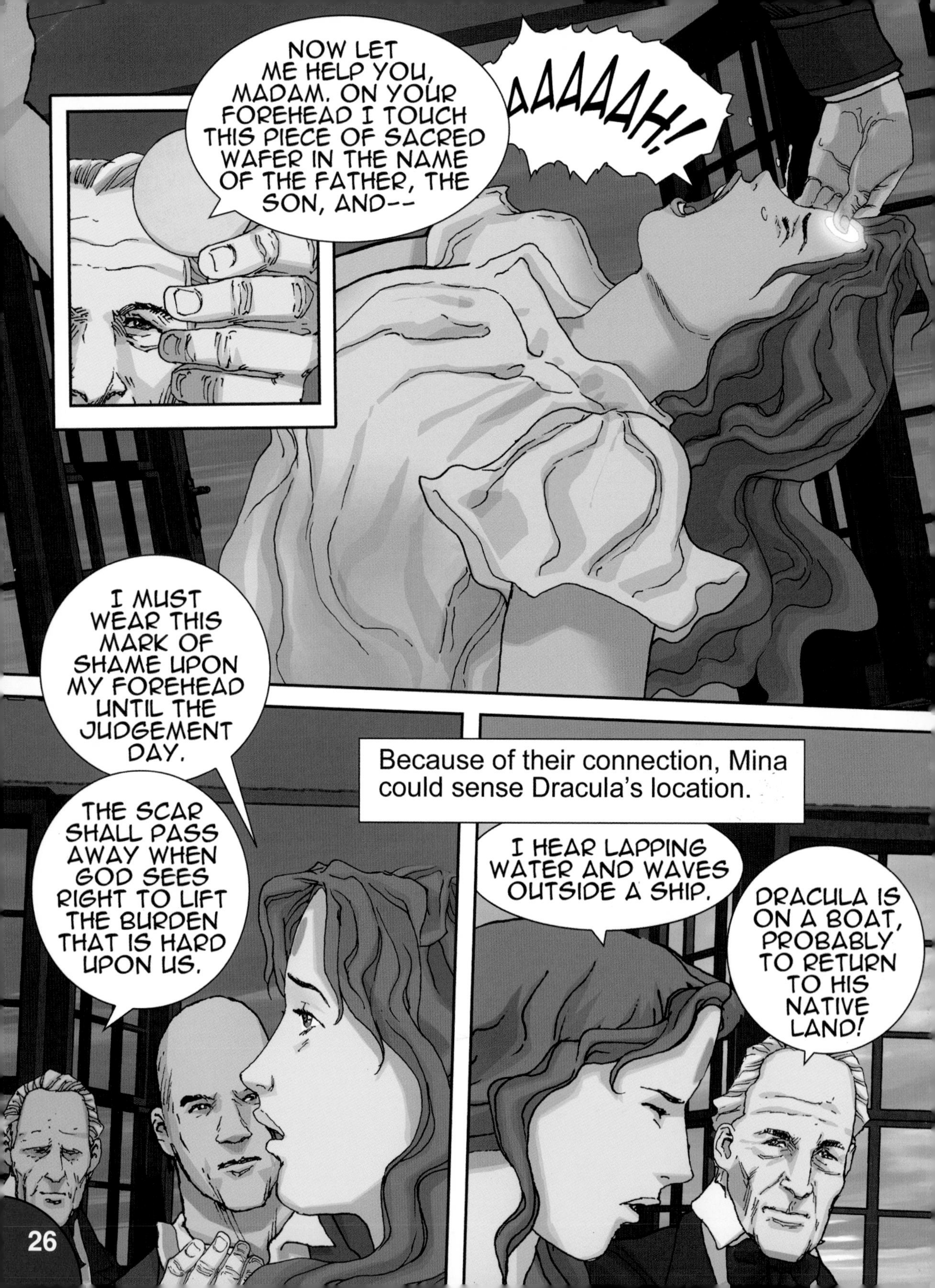
NOW LET ME HELP YOU, MADAM. ON YOUR FOREHEAD I TOUCH THIS PIECE OF SACRED WAFER IN THE NAME OF THE FATHER, THE SON, AND--
AAAAAH!
I MUST WEAR THIS MARK OF SHAME UPON MY FOREHEAD UNTIL THE JUDGEMENT DAY.
THE SCAR SHALL PASS AWAY WHEN GOD SEES RIGHT TO LIFT THE BURDEN THAT IS HARD UPON US.
Because of their connection, Mina could sense Dracula's location.
I HEAR LAPPING WATER AND WAVES OUTSIDE A SHIP.
DRACULA IS ON A BOAT, PROBABLY TO RETURN TO HIS NATIVE LAND!

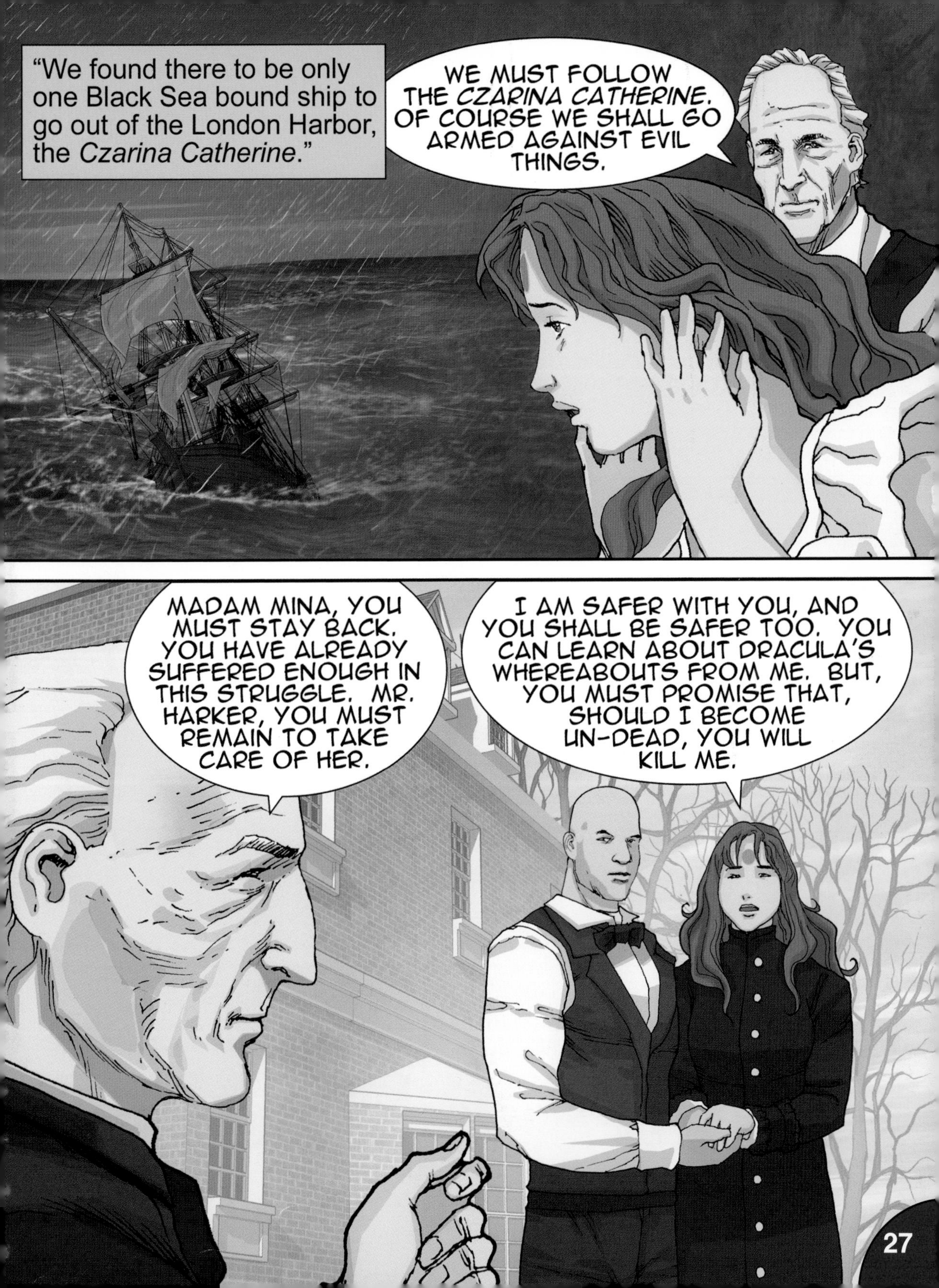
"We found there to be only one Black Sea bound ship to go out of the London Harbor, the *Czarina Catherine*."
WE MUST FOLLOW THE *CZARINA CATHERINE*. OF COURSE WE SHALL GO ARMED AGAINST EVIL THINGS.
MADAM MINA, YOU MUST STAY BACK. YOU HAVE ALREADY SUFFERED ENOUGH IN THIS STRUGGLE. MR. HARKER, YOU MUST REMAIN TO TAKE CARE OF HER.
I AM SAFER WITH YOU, AND YOU SHALL BE SAFER TOO. YOU CAN LEARN ABOUT DRACULA'S WHEREABOUTS FROM ME. BUT, YOU MUST PROMISE THAT, SHOULD I BECOME UN-DEAD, YOU WILL KILL ME.

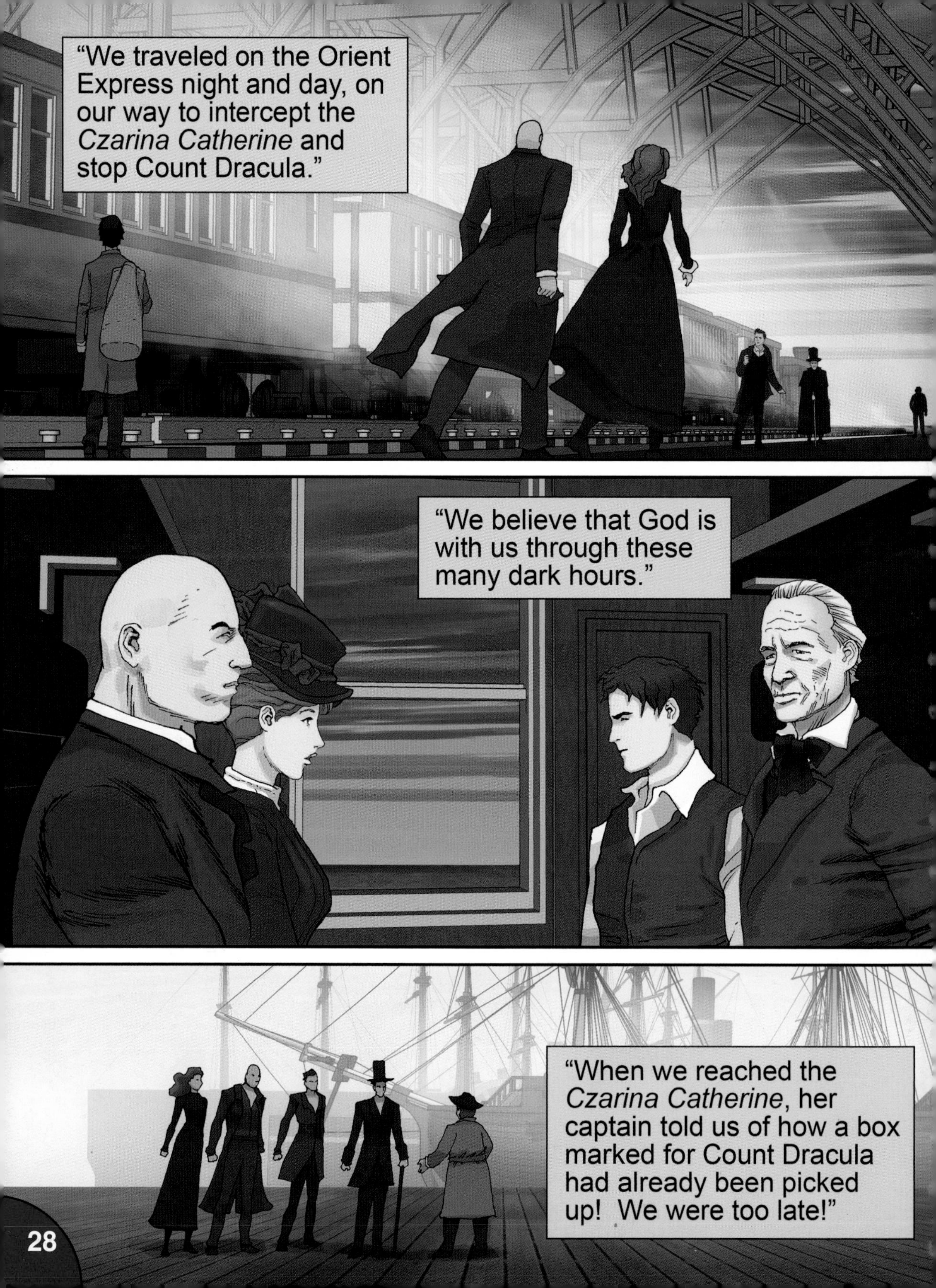
"We traveled on the Orient Express night and day, on our way to intercept the *Czarina Catherine* and stop Count Dracula."
"We believe that God is with us through these many dark hours."
"When we reached the *Czarina Catherine*, her captain told us of how a box marked for Count Dracula had already been picked up! We were too late!"

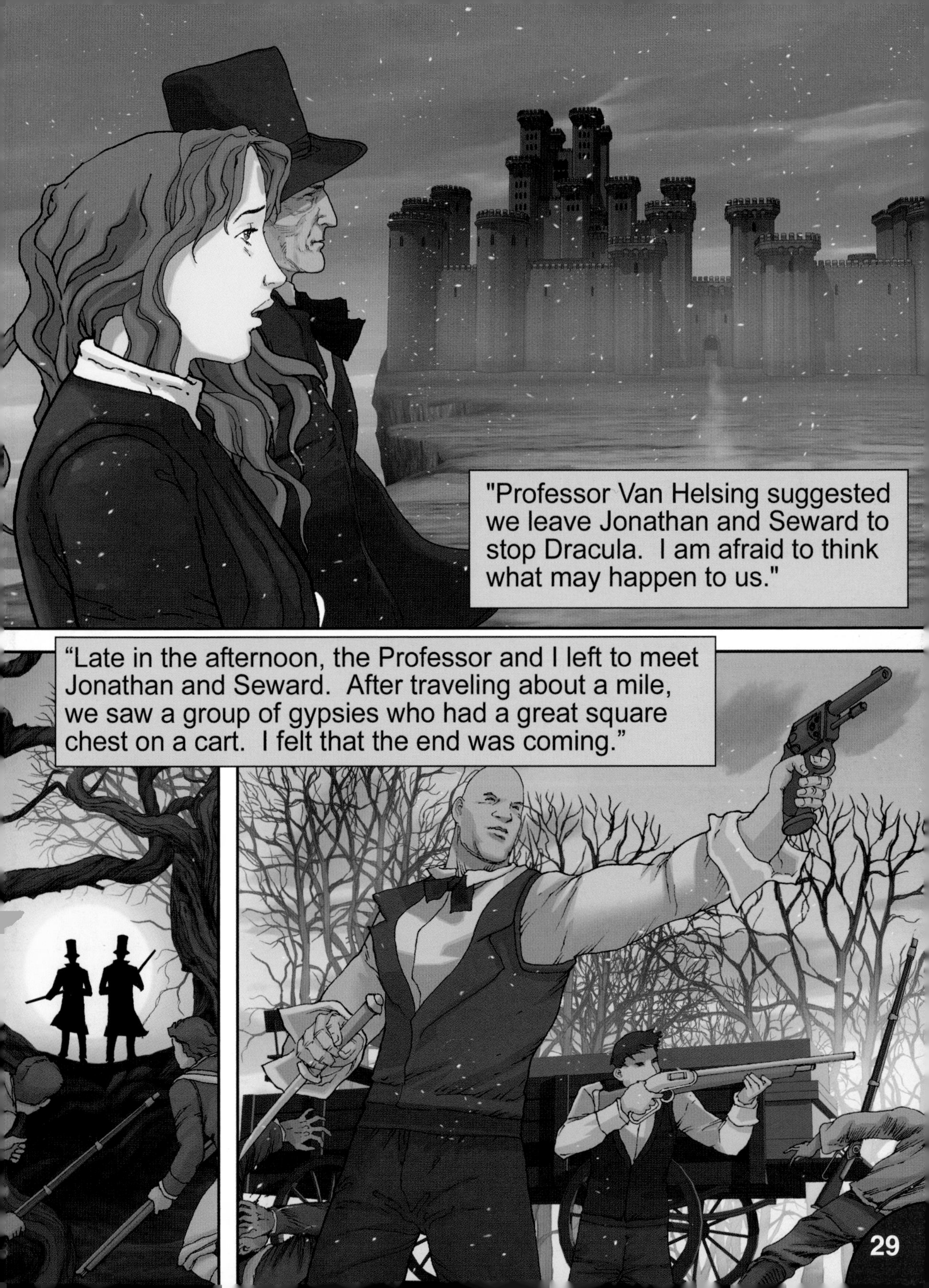
"Professor Van Helsing suggested we leave Jonathan and Seward to stop Dracula. I am afraid to think what may happen to us."
"Late in the afternoon, the Professor and I left to meet Jonathan and Seward. After traveling about a mile, we saw a group of gypsies who had a great square chest on a cart. I felt that the end was coming."

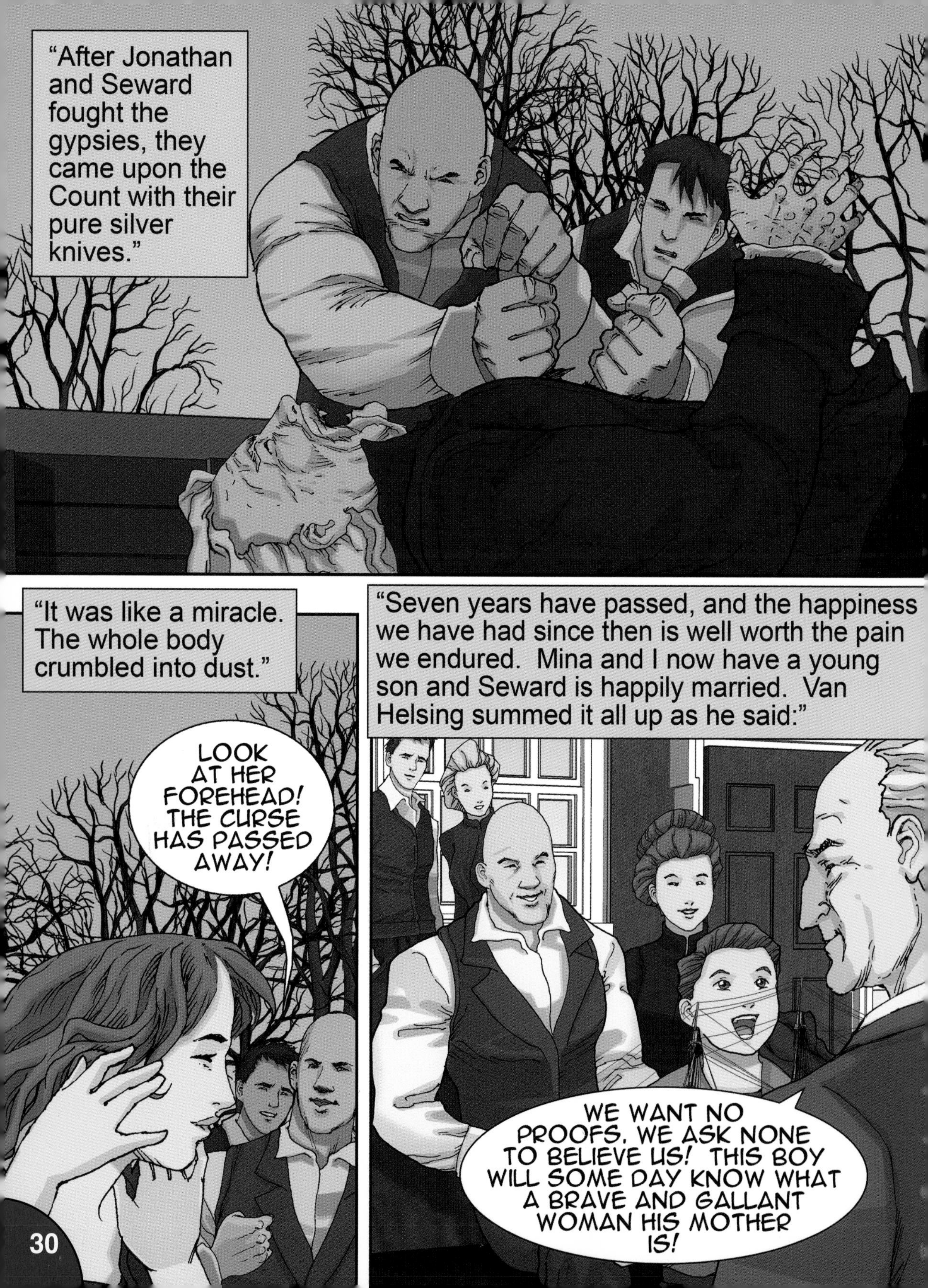
"After Jonathan and Seward fought the gypsies, they came upon the Count with their pure silver knives."
"It was like a miracle. The whole body crumbled into dust."
LOOK AT HER FOREHEAD! THE CURSE HAS PASSED AWAY!
"Seven years have passed, and the happiness we have had since then is well worth the pain we endured. Mina and I now have a young son and Seward is happily married. Van Helsing summed it all up as he said:"
WE WANT NO PROOFS. WE ASK NONE TO BELIEVE US! THIS BOY WILL SOME DAY KNOW WHAT A BRAVE AND GALLANT WOMAN HIS MOTHER IS!

About the Author

    Bram Stoker was born in Dublin, Ireland, on November 8, 1847. He was the third of seven children. Stoker was ill throughout his childhood. Because of this, he did not walk until he was seven years old.

    Stoker outgrew his illness, and he entered the University of Dublin when he was 16. He became an outstanding athlete. While he was at the University, he discovered a passion for theater.

    In 1870, Stoker began his work as a civil servant at Dublin Castle. In 1878, he met his idol, actor Sir Henry Irving. He soon accepted a job as Irving's manager. In 1878, he also married Florence Balcombe and moved to London, England.

    Stoker's first book was published in 1879. It was a handbook. He later turned to fiction, and his masterpiece, Dracula, was published in 1897. Stoker wrote several novels after, but none were as popular as Dracula. Bram Stoker died on April 20, 1912, in London. His successful novel has since been enjoyed as plays and films by people around the world.

Additional Works

The Duties of Clerks of Petty Sessions in Ireland (1879)
The Snake's Pass (1891)
Dracula (1897)
The Mystery of the Sea (1902)
The Jewel of Seven Stars (1904)
The Lady of the Shroud (1909)

Glossary

abbey – a monastery.

asylum – an institution that protects and cares for those in need, especially the mentally ill, the poor, or orphans.

count – a noble who was the governor of a county.

crucifix – a piece of art or statue showing Christ on the cross.

emaciated – having become very thin.

intercept – to interrupt the progress of something before it arrives at its destination, usually secretly.

sane – having a sound mind.

semblance – looking or seeming to resemble something.

stupor – a state of being in shock or dazed.

transfusion – to transfer, as with blood, into the vein of a person or animal.

Web Sites

To learn more about Bram Stoker, visit the ABDO Group online at **www.abdopublishing.com**. Web sites about Stoker are featured on our Book Links page. These links are routinely monitored and updated to provide the most current information available.